PROCEED WITH CAUTION...

Mr. Brennan is a sometime poet, and he brings to the weird tale the poet's incisive sensibility, the magic that provokes chills down the spine, the web of words that weaves the reader into a quivering trap of fear.

From the oozing terror of **Slime** to the nightmare of **Canavan's Back Yard**, these are tales that offer the best of Joseph Payne Brennan's early work in the macabre to readers who, however jaded, will find it difficult to forget the crawling horror that surrounds these stories like an aura.

YOU HAVE BEEN WARNED...

BY JOSEPH PAYNE BRENNAN . . .

BOOKS
Heart of Earth (Poems, 1950)
The Humming Stair (Poems, 1953)

PAMPHLETS
H. P. Lovecraft: A Bibliography (1952)
H. P. Lovecraft: An Evaluation (1955)
20,000 Feet Over History (for American Airlines, 1958)

NINE HORRORS
AND A DREAM

JOSEPH PAYNE BRENNAN

BALLANTINE BOOKS   NEW YORK

Copyright, 1958 by JOSEPH PAYNE BRENNAN

Published by arrangement with Arkham House

The Green Parrot, copyright 1952, by Weird Tales, for *Weird Tales*, July 1952. Reprinted by permission of John Schaffner.

Slime, copyright 1953, by Weird Tales, for *Weird Tales*, March 1953. Reprinted by permission of John Schaffner.

On the Elevator, copyright 1953, by Weird Tales, for *Weird Tales*, July 1953. Reprinted by permission of John Schaffner.

The Calamander Chest, copyright 1953, by Weird Tales, for *Weird Tales*, January 1954. Reprinted by permission of John Schaffner.

Death in Peru, copyright 1953, by Palmer Publications, Inc., for *Mystic Magazine*, January 1954.

I'm Murdering Mr. Massington, copyright 1954, by Esquire, Inc., for *Esquire*, February 1954. Reprinted by permission of John Schaffner.

PRINTED IN THE UNITED STATES OF AMERICA

BALLANTINE BOOKS, INC.
101 5th Avenue, New York 3, N. Y.

Contents

Slime 1

Levitation 33

The Calamander Chest 39

Death in Peru 51

On the Elevator 61

The Green Parrot 71

Canavan's Back Yard 79

I'm Murdering
   Mr. Massington 95

The Hunt 101

The Mail for Juniper Hill 113

To the Memory of *Weird Tales*
1923-1954

Slime

It was a great gray-black hood of horror moving over the floor of the sea. It slid through the soft ooze like a monstrous mantle of slime obscenely animated with questing life. It was by turns viscid and fluid. At times it flattened out and flowed through the carpet of mud like an inky pool; occasionally it paused, seeming to shrink in upon itself, and reared up out of the ooze until it resembled an irregular cone or a gigantic hood. Although it possessed no eyes, it had a marvelously developed sense of touch, and it possessed a sensitivity to minute vibrations which was almost akin to telepathy. It was plastic, essentially shapeless. It could shoot out long tentacles, until it bore a resemblance to a nightmare squid or a huge starfish; it could retract itself into a round flattened disk, or squeeze into an irregular hunched shape so that it looked like a black boulder sunk on the bottom of the sea.

It had prowled the black water endlessly. It had been formed when the earth and the seas were young; it was almost as old as the ocean itself. It moved through a night which had no beginning and no dissolution. The black sea basin where it lurked had been dark since the world began—an environment only a little less inimical than the stupendous gulfs of interplanetary space.

It was animated by a single, unceasing, never-satisfied drive: a voracious, insatiable hunger. It could survive for months without food, but minutes after eating it was as ravenous as ever. Its appetite was appalling and incalculable.

On the icy ink-black floor of the sea the battle for survival was savage, hideous—and usually brief. But for the shape of moving slime there was no battle. It ate whatever came its way, regardless of size, shape or disposition. It absorbed microscopic plankton and giant squid with equal assurance. Had its surface been less fluid, it might have retained the circular scars left by the grappling suckers of the wildly threshing deepwater squid, or the jagged toothmarks of the anachronistic frillshark, but as it was, neither left any evidence of its absorption. When the lifting curtain of living slime swayed out of the mud and closed upon them, their fiercest death throes came to nothing.

The horror did not know fear. There was nothing to be afraid of. It ate whatever moved, or tried not to move, and it had never encountered anything which could in turn eat it. If a squid's sucker, or a shark's tooth, tore into the mass of its viscosity, the rent flowed in upon itself and immediately closed. If a segment was detached, it could be retrieved and absorbed back into the whole.

The black mantle reigned supreme in its savage world of slime and silence. It groped greedily and endlessly through the mud, eating and never sleeping, never resting. If it lay still, it was only to trap food which might otherwise be lost. If it rushed with terrifying speed across the slimy bottom, it was never to escape an enemy, but always to flop its hideous fluidity upon its sole and inevitable quarry—food.

It had evolved out of the muck and slime of the primitive sea floor, and it was as alien to ordinary terrestrial life as the weird denizens of some wild

Slime

planet in a distant galaxy. It was an anachronistic experiment of nature compared to which the saber-toothed tiger, the woolly mammoth and even Tyrannosaurus, the slashing, murderous king of the great earth reptiles, were as tame, weak entities.

Had it not been for a vast volcanic upheaval on the bottom of the ocean basin, the black horror would have crept out its entire existence on the silent sea ooze without ever manifesting its hideous powers to mankind.

Fate, in the form of a violent subterranean explosion, covering huge areas of the ocean's floor, hurled it out of its black slime world and sent it spinning toward the surface.

Had it been an ordinary deep-water fish, it never would have survived the experience. The explosion itself, or the drastic lessening of water pressure as it shot toward the surface, would have destroyed it. But it was no ordinary fish. Its viscosity, or plasticity, or whatever it was that constituted its essentially amoebic structure, permitted it to survive.

It reached the surface slightly stunned and flopped on the surging waters like a great blob of black blubber. Immense waves stirred up by the subterranean explosion swept it swiftly toward shore, and because it was somewhat stunned it did not try to resist the roaring mountains of water.

Along with scattered ash, pumice and the puffed bodies of dead fish, the black horror was hurled toward a beach. The huge waves carried it more than a mile inland, far beyond the strip of sandy shore, and deposited it in the midst of a deep brackish swamp area.

As luck would have it, the submarine explosion and subsequent tidal wave took place at night, and therefore the slime horror was not immediately subjected to a new and hateful experience—light.

Although the midnight darkness of the storm-lashed swamp did not begin to compare with the stygian blackness of the sea bottom where even violet rays of the spectrum could not penetrate, the marsh darkness was nevertheless deep and intense.

As the water of the great wave receded, sluicing through the thorn jungle and back out to sea, the black horror clung to a mud bank surrounded by a rank growth of cattails. It was aware of the sudden, startling change in its environment and for some time it lay motionless, concentrating its attention on obscure internal readjustment which the absence of crushing pressure and a surrounding cloak of frigid sea water demanded. Its adaptability was incredible and horrifying. It achieved in a few hours what an ordinary creature could have attained only through a process of gradual evolution. Three hours after the titanic wave flopped it onto the mudbank, it had undergone swift organic changes which left it relatively at ease in its new environment.

In fact, it felt lighter and more mobile than it ever had before in its sea basin existence.

As it flung out feelers and attuned itself to the minutest vibrations and emanations of the swamp area, its pristine hunger drive reasserted itself with overwhelming urgency. And the tale which its sensory apparatus returned to the monstrous something which served it as a brain, excited it tremendously. It sensed at once that the swamp was filled with luscious tidbits of quivering food—more food, and food of a greater variety than it had ever encountered on the cold floor of the sea.

Its savage, incessant hunger seemed unbearable. Its

slimy mass was swept by a shuddering wave of anticipation.

Sliding off the mud bank, it slithered over the cattails into an adjacent area consisting of deep black pools interspersed with water-logged tussocks. Weed stalks stuck up out of the water and the decayed trunks of fallen trees floated half-submerged in the larger pools.

Ravenous with hunger, it sloshed into the bog area, flicking its fluid tentacles about. Within minutes it had snatched up several fat frogs and a number of small fish. These, however, merely titillated its appetite. Its hunger turned into a kind of ecstatic fury. It commenced a systematic hunt, plunging to the bottom of each pool and quickly but carefully exploring every inch of its oozy bottom. The first creature of any size which it encountered was a muskrat. An immense curtain of adhesive slime suddenly swept out of the darkness, closed upon it—and squeezed.

Heartened and whetted by its find, the hood of horror rummaged the rank pools with renewed zeal. When it surfaced, it carefully probed the tussocks for anything that might have escaped it in the water. Once it snatched up a small bird nesting in some swamp grass. Occasionally it slithered up the criss-crossed trunks of fallen trees, bearing them down with its unspeakable slimy bulk, and hung briefly suspended like a great dripping curtain of black marsh mud.

It was approaching a somewhat less swampy and more deeply wooded area when it gradually became aware of a subtle change in its new environment. It paused, hesitating, and remained half in and half out of a small pond near the edge of the nearest trees.

Although it had absorbed twenty-five or thirty pounds of food in the form of frogs, fish, water snakes, the muskrat and a few smaller creatures, its fierce hunger had not left it. Its monstrous appetite urged it on, and yet something held it anchored in the pond.

What it sensed, but could not literally see, was the rising sun spreading a gray light over the swamp. The horror had never encountered any illumination except that generated by the grotesque phosphorescent appendages of various deep-sea fishes. Natural light was totally unknown to it.

As the dawn light strengthened, breaking through the scattering storm clouds, the black slime monster fresh from the inky floor of the sea sensed that something utterly unknown was flooding in upon it. Light was hateful to it. It cast out quick feelers, hoping to catch and crush the light. But the more frenzied its efforts became, the more intense became the abhorred aura surrounding it.

At length, as the sun rose visibly above the trees, the horror, in baffled rage rather than in fear, grudgingly slid back into the pond and burrowed into the soft ooze of its bottom. There it remained while the sun shone and the small creatures of the swamp ventured forth on furtive errands.

A few miles away from Wharton's Swamp, in the small town of Clinton Center, Henry Hossing sleepily crawled out of the improvised alley shack which had afforded him a degree of shelter for the night and stumbled into the street. Passing a hand across his rheumy eyes, he scratched the stubble on his cheek and blinked listlessly at the rising sun. He had not slept well; the storm of the night before had kept him awake. Besides he had gone to bed hungry, and that never agreed with him.

Glancing furtively along the street, he walked

Slime

slouched forward, with his head bent down, and most of the time he kept his eyes on the walk or on the gutter in the hopes of spotting a chance coin.

Clinton Center had not been kind to him. The handouts were sparse, and only yesterday he had been warned out of town by one of the local policemen.

Grumbling to himself, he reached the end of the street and started to cross. Suddenly he stooped quickly and snatched up something from the edge of the pavement.

It was a crumpled green bill, and as he frantically unfolded it, a look of stupefied rapture spread across his bristly face. Ten dollars! More money than he had possessed at any one time in months!

Stowing it carefully in the one good pocket of his seedy gray jacket, he crossed the street with a swift stride. Instead of sweeping the sidewalks, his eyes now darted along the rows of stores and restaurants.

He paused at one restaurant, hesitated, and finally went on until he found another less pretentious one a few blocks away.

When he sat down, the counterman shook his head. "Get goin', bud. No free coffee today."

With a wide grin, the hobo produced his ten-dollar bill and spread it on the counter. "That covers a good breakfast here, pardner?"

The counterman seemed irritated. "O.K. O.K. What'll you have?" He eyed the bill suspiciously.

Henry Hossing ordered orange juice, toast, ham and eggs, oatmeal, melon and coffee.

When it appeared, he ate every bit of it, ordered three additional cups of coffee, paid the check as if two-dollar breakfasts were customary with him, and then sauntered back to the street.

Shortly after noon, after his three-dollar lunch, he

saw the liquor store. For a few minutes he stood across the street from it, fingering his five-dollar bill. Finally he crossed with an abstracted smile, entered and bought a quart of rye.

He hesitated on the sidewalk, debating whether or not he should return to the little shack in the side alley. After a minute or two of indecision, he decided against it and struck out instead for Wharton's Swamp. The local police were far less likely to disturb him there, and since the skies were clearing and the weather mild, there was little immediate need of shelter.

Angling off the highway which skirted the swamp several miles from town, he crossed a marshy meadow, pushed through a fringe of brush and sat down under a sweet-gum tree which bordered a deeply wooded area.

By late afternoon he had achieved a quite cheerful glow, and he had little inclination to return to Clinton Center. Rousing himself from reverie, he stumbled about collecting enough wood for a small fire and went back to his sylvan seat under the sweet-gum.

He slept briefly as dusk descended, but finally bestirred himself again to build a fire, as deeper shadows fell over the swamp. Then he returned to his swiftly diminishing bottle. He was suspended in a warm net of inflamed fantasy when something abruptly broke the spell and brought him back to earth.

The flickering flames of his fire had dwindled down until now only a dim eerie glow illuminated the immediate area under the sweet-gum. He saw nothing and at the moment heard nothing and yet he was filled with a sudden and profound sense of lurking menace.

He stood up, staggering, leaned back against the sweet-gum and peered fearfully into the shadows. In the deep darkness beyond the waning arc of firelight

Slime

he could distinguish nothing which had any discernible form or color.

Then he detected the stench and shuddered. In spite of the reek of cheap whiskey which clung around him, the smell was overpowering. It was a heavy, fulsome fetid, alien and utterly repellent. It was vaguely fish-like, but otherwise beyond any known comparison.

As he stood trembling under the sweet-gum, Henry Hossing thought of something dead which had lain for long ages at the bottom of the sea.

Filled with mounting alarm, he looked around for some wood which he might add to the dying fire. All he could find nearby however were a few twigs. He threw these on and the flames licked up briefly and subsided.

He listened and heard—or imagined he heard—an odd sort of slithering sound in the nearby bushes. It seemed to retreat slightly as the flames shot up.

Genuine terror took possession of him. He knew that he was in no condition to flee—and now he came to the horrifying conclusion that whatever unspeakable menace waited in the surrounding darkness was temporarily held at bay only by the failing gleam of his little fire.

Frantically he looked around for more wood. But there was none. None, that is, within the faint glow of firelight. And he dared not venture beyond.

He began to tremble uncontrollably. He tried to scream but no sound came out of tightened throat.

The ghastly stench became stronger, and now he was sure that he could hear a strange sliding, slithering sound in the black shadows beyond the remaining spark of firelight.

He stood frozen in absolute helpless panic as the tiny fire smouldered down into darkness.

Nine Horrors and a Dream

At the last instant a charred bit of wood broke apart, sending up a few sparks, and in that flicker of final light he glimpsed the horror.

It had already glided out of the bushes and now it rushed across the small clearing with nightmare speed. It was a final incarnation of all the fears, shuddering apprehensions and bad dreams which Henry Hossing had ever known in his life. It was a fiend from the pit of Hell come to claim him at last.

A terrible ringing scream burst from his throat, but it was smothered before it was finished as the black shape of slime fastened upon him with irresistible force.

Giles Gowse—"Old Man" Gowse—got out of bed after eight hours of fitful tossing and intermittent nightmares and grouchily brewed coffee in the kitchen of his dilapidated farmhouse on the edge of Wharton's Swamp. Half the night, it seemed, the stench of stale sea-water had permeated the house. His interrupted sleep had been full of foreboding, full of shadowy and evil portents.

Muttering to himself, he finished breakfast, took a milk pail from the pantry and started for the barn where he kept his single cow.

As he approached the barn, the strange offensive odor which had plagued him during the night assailed his nostrils anew.

"Wharton's Swamp! That's what it is!" he told himself. And he shook his fist at it.

When he entered the barn the stench was stronger than ever. Scowling, he strode toward the rickety stall where he kept the cow, Sarey.

Then he stood still and stared. Sarey was gone. The stall was empty.

Slime

He reentered the barnyard. "Sarey!" he called.

Rushing back into the barn, he inspected the stall. The rancid reek of the sea was strong here and now he noticed a kind of shine on the floor. Bending closer, he saw that it was a slick coat of glistening slime, as if some unspeakable creature covered with ooze had crept in and out of the stall.

This discovery, coupled with the weird disappearance of Sarey, was too much for his jangled nerves. With a wild yell he ran out of the barn and started for Clinton Center, two miles away.

His reception in the town enraged him. When he tried to tell people about the disappearance of his cow, Sarey, about the reek of sea and ooze in his barn the night before they laughed at him. The more impolite ones, that is. Most of the others patiently heard him out—and then winked and touched their heads significantly when he was out of sight.

One man, the druggist, Jim Jelinson, seemed mildly interested. He said that as he was coming through his backyard from the garage late the previous evening, he had heard a fearful shriek somewhere in the distant darkness. It might, he averred, have come from the direction of Wharton's Swamp. But it had not been repeated and eventually he had dismissed it from his mind.

When Old Man Gowse started for home late in the afternoon he was filled with sullen, resentful bitterness. They thought he was crazy, eh? Well, Sarey *was* gone; they couldn't explain *that* away, could they? They explained the smell by saying it was dead fish cast up by the big wave which had washed into the swamp during the storm. Well—maybe. And the slime on his barn floor they said was snails. *Snails!* As if any he'd ever seen could cause that much slime!

As he was nearing home, he met Rupert Barnaby, his nearest neighbor. Rupert was carrying a rifle and he was accompanied by Jibbe, his hound.

Although there had been an element of bad blood between the two bachelor neighbors for some time, Old Man Gowse, much to Barnaby's surprise, nodded and stopped'

"Evenin' hunt, neighbor?"

Barnaby nodded. "Thought Jibbe might start up a coon. Moon later, likely."

"My cow's gone," Old Man Gowse said abruptly. "If you should see her—" He paused. "But I don't think you will. . . ."

Barnaby, bewildered, stared at him. "What you gettin' at?"

Old Man Gowse repeated what he had been telling all day in Clinton Center.

He shook his head when he finished, adding. "I wouldn't go huntin' in that swamp tonight fur—ten thousand dollars!"

Rupert Barnaby threw back his head and laughed. He was a big man, muscular, resourceful and level-headed—little given to even mild flights of the imagination.

"Gowse," he laughed, "no use you givin' me those spook stories! Your cow just got loose and wandered off. Why, I ain't even seen a bobcat in that swamp for over a year!"

Old Man Gowse set his lips in a grim line. "Maybe," he said, as he turned away, "you'll see suthin' worse than a wildcat in that swamp tonight!"

Shaking his head, Barnaby took after his impatient hound. Old Man Gowse was getting queer all right. One of these days he'd probably go off altogether and have to be locked up.

Slime

Jibbe ran ahead, sniffing, darting from one ditch to another. As twilight closed in, Barnaby angled off the main road onto a twisting path which led into Wharton's Swamp.

He loved hunting. He would rather tramp through the brush than sit home in an easy chair. And even if an evening's foray turned up nothing, he didn't particularly mind. Actually he made out quite well; at least half his meat supply consisted of the rabbits, racoons and occasional deer which he brought down in Wharton's Swamp.

When the moon rose, he was deep in the swamp. Twice Jibbe started off after rabbits, but both times he returned quickly, looking somewhat sheepish.

Something about his actions began to puzzle Barnaby. The dog seemed reluctant to move ahead; he hung directly in front of the hunter. Once Barnaby tripped over him and nearly fell headlong.

The hunter paused finally, frowning, and looked ahead. The swamp appeared no different than usual. True, a rather offensive stench hung over it, but that was merely the result of the big waves which had splashed far inland during the recent storm. Probably an accumulation of seaweed and the decaying bodies of some dead fish lay rotting in the stagnant pools of the swamp.

Barnaby spoke sharply to the dog. "What ails you, boy? Git now! You trip me again, you'll get a boot!"

The dog started ahead some distance, but with an air of reluctance. He sniffed the clumps of marsh grass in a perfunctory manner and seemed to have lost interest in the hunt.

Barnaby grew exasperated. Even when they discovered the fresh track of a racoon in the soft mud near a little pool, Jibbe manifested only slight interest.

He did run on ahead a little further however, and Barnaby began to hope that, as they closed in, he would regain his customary enthusiasm.

In this he was mistaken. As they approached a thickly wooded area, latticed with tree thorns and covered with a heavy growth of cattails, the dog suddenly crouched in the shadows and refused to budge.

Barnaby was sure that the racoon had taken refuge in the nearby thickets. The dog's unheard of conduct infuriated him.

After a number of sharp cuffs, Jibbe arose stiffly and moved ahead, the hair on his neck bristled up like a lion's mane.

Swearing to himself, Barnaby pushed into the darkened thickets after him.

It was quite black under the trees, in spite of the moonlight, and he moved cautiously in order to avoid stepping into a pool.

Suddenly, with a frantic yelp of terror, Jibbe literally darted between his legs and shot out of the thickets. He ran on, howling weirdly as he went.

For the first time that evening Barnaby experienced a thrill of fear. In all his previous experience, Jibbe had never turned tail. On one occasion he had even plunged in after a sizeable bear.

Scowling into the deep darkness, Barnaby could see nothing. There were no baleful eyes glaring at him.

As his own eyes tried to penetrate the surrounding blackness, he recalled Old Man Gowse's warning with a bitter grimace. If the old fool happened to spot Jibbe streaking out of the swamp, Barnaby would never hear the end of it.

The thought of this angered him. He pushed ahead now with a feeling of sullen rage for whatever had

Slime

terrified the dog. A good rifle shot would solve the mystery.

All at once he stopped and listened. From the darkness immediately ahead, he detected an odd sound, as if a large bulk were being dragged over the cattails.

He hesitated, unable to see anything, stoutly resisting an idiotic impulse to flee. The black darkness and the slimy stench of stagnant pools here in the thickets seemed to be suffocating him.

His heart began to pound as the slithering noise came closer. Every instinct told him to turn and run, but a kind of desperate stubbornness held him rooted to the spot.

The sound grew louder and suddenly he was positive that something deadly and formidable was rushing toward him through the thickets with accelerated speed.

Throwing up his rifle, he pointed at the direction of the sound and fired.

In the brief flash of the rifle he saw something black and enormous and glistening, like a great flapping hood, break through the final thicket. It seemed to be *rolling* toward him, and it was moving with nightmare swiftness.

He wanted to scream and run, but even as the horror rushed forward, he understood that flight at this point would be futile. Even though the blood seemed to have congealed in his veins, he held the rifle pointed up and kept on firing.

The shots had no more visible effect than so many pebbles launched from a slingshot. At the last instant his nerve broke and he tried to escape, but the monstrous hood lunged upon him, flapped over him and squeezed, and his attempt at a scream turned into a tiny gurgle in his throat.

Nine Horrors and a Dream

Old Man Gowse got up early, after another uneasy night, and walked out to inspect the barnyard area. Nothing further seemed amiss, but there was still no sign of Sarey. And that detestable odor arose from the direction of Wharton's Swamp when the wind was right.

After breakfast, Gowse set out for Rupert Barnaby's place, a mile or so distant along the road. He wasn't sure himself what he expected to find.

When he reached Barnaby's small but neat frame house, all was quiet. Too quiet. Usually Barnaby was up and about soon after sunrise.

On a sudden impulse, Gowse walked up the path and rapped on the front door. He waited and there was no reply. He knocked again, and after another pause, stepped off the porch.

Jibbe, Barnaby's hound, slunk around the side of the house. Ordinarily he would bound about and bark. But today he stood motionless—or nearly so—he was trembling—and stared at Gowse. The dog had a cowed, frightened, guilty air which was entirely alien to him.

"Where's Rup?" Gowse called to him. "Go get Rup!"

Instead of starting off, the dog threw back his head and emitted an eerie, long-drawn howl.

Gowse shivered. With a backward glance at the silent house, he started off down the road.

Now maybe they'd listen to him, he thought grimly. The day before they had laughed about the disappearance of Sarey. Maybe they wouldn't laugh so easily when he told them that Rupert Barnaby had gone into Wharton's Swamp with his dog—and that the dog had come back alone!

When Police Chief Miles Underbeck saw Old Man

Slime

Gowse come into headquarters in Clinton Center, he sat back and sighed heavily. He was busy this morning and undoubtedly Old Man Gowse was coming in to inquire about the infernal cow of his that had wandered off.

The old eccentric had a new and startling report, however. He claimed that Rupert Barnaby was missing. He'd gone into the swamp the night before, Gowse insisted, and had not returned.

When Chief Underbeck questioned him closely, Gowse admitted that he wasn't *positive* Barnaby hadn't returned. It was barely possible that he had returned home very early in the morning and then left again before Gowse arrived.

But Gowse fixed his flashing eyes on the Chief and shook his head. "He never came out, I tell ye! That dog of his knows! Howled, he did, like a dog howls for the dead! Whatever come took Sarey—got Barnaby in the swamp last night!"

Chief Underbeck was not an excitable man. Gowse's burst of melodrama irritated him and left him unimpressed.

Somewhat gruffly he promised to look into the matter if Barnaby had not turned up by evening. Barnaby, he pointed out, knew the swamp better than anyone else in the county. And he was perfectly capable of taking care of himself. Probably, the Chief suggested, he had sent the dog home and gone elsewhere after finishing his hunt the evening before. The chances were he'd be back by suppertime.

Old Man Gowse shook his head with a kind of fatalistic skepticism. Vouching that events would soon prove his fears well founded, he shambled grouchily out of the station.

The day passed and there was no sign of Rupert

Barnaby. At six o'clock, Old Man Gowse grimly marched into the Crown, Clinton Center's second-rung hotel, and registered for a room. At seven o'clock Chief Underbeck dispatched a prowl car to Barnaby's place. He waited impatiently for its return, drumming on the desk, disinterestedly shuffling through a sheaf of reports which had accumulated during the day.

The prowl car returned shortly before eight. Sergeant Grimes made his report. "Nobody there, sir. Place locked up tight. Searched the grounds. All we saw was Barnaby's dog. Howled and ran off as if the devil were on his tail!"

Chief Underbeck was troubled. If Barnaby *was* missing, a search should be started at once. But it was already getting dark, and portions of Wharton's Swamp were very nearly impassable even during the day. Besides, there was no proof that Barnaby had not gone off for a visit, perhaps to nearby Stantonville, for instance, to call on a crony and stay overnight.

By nine o'clock he had decided to postpone any action till morning. A search now would probably be futile in any case. The swamp offered too many obstacles. If Barnaby had not turned up by morning, and there was no report that he had been seen elsewhere, a systematic search of the marsh could begin.

Not long after he had arrived at this decision, and as he was somewhat wearily preparing to leave Headquarters and go home, a new and genuinely alarming interruption took place.

Shortly before nine-thirty, a car braked to a sudden stop outside Headquarters. An elderly man hurried in, supporting by the arm a sobbing, hysterical young girl. Her skirt and stockings were torn and there were a number of scratches on her face.

After assisting her to a chair, the man turned to

Slime

Chief Underbeck and the other officers who gathered around.

"Picked her up on the highway out near Wharton's Swamp. Screaming at the top of her lungs!" He wiped his forehead. "She ran right in front of my car. Missed her by a miracle. She was so crazy with fear I couldn't make sense out of what she said. Seems like something grabbed her boy friend in the bushes out there. Anyway, I got her in the car without much trouble and I guess I broke a speed law getting here."

Chief Underbeck surveyed the man keenly. He was obviously shaken himself, and since he did not appear to be concealing anything, the Chief turned to the girl.

He spoke soothingly, doing his best to reassure her, and at length she composed herself sufficiently to tell her story.

Her name was Dolores Rell and she lived in nearby Stantonville. Earlier in the evening she had gone riding with her fiance, Jason Bukmeist of Clinton Center. As Jason was driving along the highway adjacent to Wharton's Swamp, she had remarked that the early evening moonlight looked very romantic over the marsh. Jason had stopped the car, and after they had surveyed the scene for some minutes, he suggested that since the evening was warm, a brief "stroll in the moonlight" might be fun.

Dolores had been reluctant to leave the car, but at length had been persuaded to take a short walk along the edge of the marsh where the terrain was relatively firm.

As the couple were walking along under the trees, perhaps twenty yards or so from the car, Dolores became aware of an unpleasant odor and wanted to turn back. Jason, however, told her she only imagined it and insisted on going further. As the trees grew closer together, they walked Indian file, Jason taking the lead.

Suddenly, she said, they both heard something swishing through the brush toward them. Jason told her not to be frightened, that it was probably someone's cow. As it came closer, however, it seemed to be moving with incredible speed. And it didn't seem to be making the kind of noise a cow would make.

At the last second Jason whirled with a cry of fear and told her to run. Before she could move, she saw a monstrous something rushing under the trees in the dim moonlight. For an instant she stood rooted with horror; then she turned and ran. She thought she heard Jason running behind her. She couldn't be sure. But immediately after she heard him scream.

In spite of her terror, she turned and looked behind her.

At this point in her story she became hysterical again and several minutes passed before she could go on.

She could not describe exactly what she had seen as she looked over her shoulder. The thing which she had glimpsed rushing under the trees had caught up with Jason. It almost completely covered him. All she could see of him was his agonized face and part of one arm, low near the ground, as if the thing were squatting astride him. She could not say what it was. It was black, formless, bestial and yet not bestial. It was the dark gliding kind of indescribable horror which she had shuddered at when she was a little girl alone in the nursery at night.

She shuddered now and covered her eyes as she tried to picture what she had seen. "O God—*the darkness came alive! The darkness came alive!*"

Somehow, she went on presently, she had stumbled

Slime

through the trees into the road. She was so terrified she hardly noticed the approaching car.

There could be no doubt that Dolores Rell was in the grip of genuine terror. Chief Underbeck acted with alacrity. After the white-faced girl had been driven to a nearby hospital for treatment of her scratches and the administration of a sedative, Underbeck rounded up all available men on the force, equipped them with shotguns, rifles and flashlights, hurried them into four prowl cars and started off for Wharton's Swamp.

Jason Bukmeist's car was found where he had parked it. It had not been disturbed. A search of the nearby swamp area, conducted in the glare of flashlights, proved fruitless. Whatever had attacked Bukmeist had apparently carried him off into the farthest recesses of the sprawling swamp.

After two futile hours of brush breaking and marsh sloshing, Chief Underbeck wearily rounded up his men and called off the hunt until morning.

As the first faint streaks of dawn appeared in the sky over Wharton's Swamp, the search began again. Reinforcements, including civilian volunteers from Clinton Center, had arrived, and a systematic combing of the entire swamp commenced.

By noon, the search had proved fruitless—or nearly so. One of the searchers brought in a battered hat and a rye whiskey bottle which he had discovered on the edge of the marsh under a sweet-gum tree. The shapeless felt hat was old and worn, but it was dry. It had, therefore, apparently been discarded in the swamp since the storm of a few days ago. The whiskey bottle looked new; in fact, a few drops of rye remained in it. The searcher reported that the remains of a small campfire were also found under the sweet-gum.

In the hope that this evidence might have some

bearing on the disappearance of Jason Bukmeist, Chief Underbeck ordered a canvass of every liquor store in Clinton Center in an attempt to learn the names of everyone who had recently purchased a bottle of the particular brand of rye found under the tree.

The search went on, and mid-afternoon brought another, more ominous discovery. A diligent searcher, investigating a trampled area in a large growth of cattails, picked a rifle out of the mud.

After the slime and dirt had been wiped away, two of the searchers vouched that it belonged to Rupert Barnaby. One of them had hunted with him and remembered a bit of scrollwork on the rifle stock.

While Chief Underbeck was weighing this unpalatable bit of evidence, a report of the liquor store canvass in Clinton Center arrived. Every recent purchaser of a quart bottle of the particular brand in question had been investigated. Only one could not be located —a tramp who had hung around the town for several days and had been ordered out.

By evening most of the exhausted searching party were convinced that the tramp, probably in a state of homicidal viciousness brought on by drink, had murdered both Rupert Barnaby and Jason and secreted their bodies in one of the deep pools of the swamp. The chances were the murderer was still sleeping off the effects of drink somewhere in the tangled thickets of the marsh.

Most of the searchers regarded Dolores Rell's melodramatic story with a great deal of skepticism. In the dim moonlight, they pointed out, a frenzied, wild-eyed tramp bent on imminent murder might very well have resembled some kind of monster. And the girl's hysteria had probably magnified what she had seen.

As night closed over the dismal morass, Chief Under-

Slime

beck reluctantly suspended the hunt. In view of the fact that the murderer probably still lurked in the woods, however, he decided to establish a system of night-long patrols along the highway which paralleled the swamp. If the quarry lay hidden in the treacherous tangle of trees and brush, he would not be able to escape onto the highway without running into one of the patrols. The only other means of egress from the swamp lay miles across the mire where the open sea washed against a reedy beach. And it was quite unlikely that the fugitive would even attempt escape in that direction.

The patrols were established in three hour shifts, two men to a patrol, both heavily armed and both equipped with powerful searchlights. They were ordered to investigate every sound or movement which they detected in the brush bordering the highway. After a single command to halt, they were to shoot to kill. Any curious motorists who stopped to inquire about the hunt were to be swiftly waved on their way, after being warned not to give rides to anyone and to report all hitchhikers.

Fred Storr and Luke Matson, on the midnight to three o'clock patrol, passed an uneventful two hours on their particular stretch of the highway. Matson finally sat down on a fallen tree stump a few yards from the edge of the road.

"Legs givin' out," he commented wryly, resting his rifle on the stump. "Might as well sit a few minutes."

Fred Storr lingered nearby. "Guess so, Luke. Don't look like—" Suddenly he scowled into the black fringes of the swamp. "You hear something, Luke?"

Luke listened, twisting around on the stump. "Well, maybe," he said finally, "kind of a little scratchy sound like."

He got up, retrieving his rifle.

"Let's take a look," Fred suggested in a low voice. He stepped over the stump and Luke followed him toward the tangle of brush which marked the border of the swamp jungle.

Several yards further along they stopped again. The sound became more audible. It was a kind of slithering, scraping sound, such as might be produced by a heavy body dragging itself over uneven ground.

"Sounds like—a snake," Luke ventured. "A damn big snake!"

"We'll get a little closer," Fred whispered. "You be ready with that gun when I switch on my light!"

They moved ahead a few more yards. Then a powerful yellow ray stabbed into the thickets ahead as Fred switched on his flashlight. The ray searched the darkness, probing in one direction and then another.

Luke lowered his rifle a little, frowning. "Don't see a thing," he said. "Nothing but a big pool of black scum up ahead there."

Before Fred had time to reply, the pool of black scum reared up into horrible life. In one hideous second it hunched itself into an unspeakable glistening hood and rolled forward with fearful speed.

Luke Matson screamed and fired simultaneously as the monstrous scarf of slime shot forward. A moment later it swayed above him. He fired again and the thing fell upon him.

In avoiding the initial rush of the horror, Fred Storr lost his footing. He fell headlong—and turned just in time to witness a sight which slowed the blood in his veins.

The monster had pounced upon Luke Matson. Now, as Fred watched, literally paralyzed with horror, it spread itself over and around the form of Luke until

Slime

he was completely enveloped. The faint writhing of his limbs could still be seen. Then the thing squeezed, swelling into a hood and flattening itself again, and the writhing ceased.

As soon as the thing lifted and swung forward in his direction, Fred Storr, goaded by frantic fear, overcame the paralysis of horror which had frozen him.

Grabbing the rifle which had fallen beside him, he aimed it at the shape of living slime and started firing. Pure terror possessed him as he saw that the shots were having no effect. The thing lunged toward him, to all visible appearances entirely oblivious to the rifle slugs tearing into its loathsome viscid mass.

Acting out of some instinct which he himself could not have named, Fred Storr dropped the rifle and seized his flashlight, playing its powerful beam directly upon the onrushing horror.

The thing stopped, scant feet away, and appeared to hesitate. It slid quickly aside at an angle, but he followed it immediately with the cone of light. It backed up finally and flattened out, as if trying by that means to avoid the light, but he trained the beam on it steadily, sensing with every primitive fiber which he possessed that the yellow shaft of light was the one thing which held off hideous death.

Now there were shouts in the nearby darkness and other lights began stabbing the shadows. Members of the adjacent patrols, alarmed by the sound of rifle fire, had come running to investigate.

Suddenly the nameless horror squirmed quickly out of the flashlight's beam and rushed away in the darkness.

In the leaden light of early dawn Chief Underbeck climbed into a police car waiting on the highway near

Wharton's Swamp and headed back for Clinton Center. He had made a decision and he was grimly determined to act on it at once.

When he reached Headquarters, he made two telephone calls in quick succession, one to the governor of the state and the other to the commander of the nearby Camp Evans Military Reservation.

The horror in Wharton's Swamp—he had decided —could not be coped with by the limited men and resources at his command.

Rupert Barnaby, Jason Bukmeist and Luke Matson had without any doubt perished in the swamp. The anonymous tramp, it now began to appear, far from being the murderer, had been only one more victim. And Fred Storr—well, he hadn't disappeared. But the other patrol members had found him sitting on the ground near the edge of the swamp in the clutches of a mind-warping fear which had, temporarily at least, reduced him to near idiocy. Hours after he had been taken home and put to bed, he had refused to loosen his grip on a flashlight which he squeezed in one hand. When they switched the flashlight off, he screamed, and they had to switch it on again. His story was so wildly melodramatic it could scarcely be accepted by rational minds. And yet—they had said as much about Dolores Rell's hysterical account. And Fred Storr was no excitable young girl; he had a reputation for level-headedness, stolidity and verbal honesty which was touched with understatement rather than exaggeration. As Chief Underbeck arose and walked out to his car in order to start back to Wharton's Swamp, he noticed Old Man Gowse coming down the block.

With a sudden thrill of horror he remembered the eccentric's missing cow. Before the old man came abreast, he slammed the car door and issued crisp

Slime

directions to the waiting driver. As the car sped away, he glanced in the rear-view mirror.

Old Man Gowse stood grimly motionless on the walk in front of Police Headquarters.

"Old Man Cassandra," Chief Underbeck muttered. The driver shot a swift glance at him and stepped on the gas.

Less than two hours after Chief Underbeck arrived back at Wharton's Swamp, the adjacent highway was crowded with cars—state police patrol cars, cars of the local curious and Army trucks from Camp Evans.

Promptly at nine o'clock over three hundred soldiers, police and citizen volunteers, all armed, swung into the swamp to begin a careful search.

Shortly before dusk most of them had arrived at the sea on the far side of the swamp. Their exhaustive efforts had netted nothing. One soldier, noticing fierce eyes glaring out of a tree, had bagged an owl, and one of the state policemen had flushed a young bobcat. Someone else had stepped on a copperhead and been treated for snakebite. But there was no sign of a monster, a murderous tramp, nor any of the missing men.

In the face of mounting skepticism, Chief Underbeck stood firm. Pointing out that so far as they knew to date, the murderer prowled only at night, he ordered that after a four-hour rest and meal period the search should continue.

A number of helicopters which had hovered over the area during the afternoon landed on the strip of shore, bringing food and supplies. At Chief Underbeck's insistence, barriers were set up on the beach. Guards were stationed along the entire length of the highway; powerful searchlights were brought up. Another truck from Camp Evans arrived with a portable machine-gun and several flame-throwers.

By eleven o'clock that night the stage was set. The beach barriers were in place, guards were at station, and huge searchlights, erected near the highway, swept the dismal marsh with probing cones of light.

At eleven-fifteen the night patrols, each consisting of ten strongly-armed men, struck into the swamp again.

Ravenous with hunger, the hood of horror reared out of the mud at the bottom of a rancid pool and rose toward the surface. Flopping ashore in the darkness, it slid quickly away over the clumps of scattered swamp grass. It was impelled, as always, by a savage and enormous hunger.

Although hunting in its new environment had been good, its immense appetite knew no appeasement. The more food it consumed, the more it seemed to require.

As it rushed off, alert to the minute vibrations which indicated food, it became aware of various disturbing emanations. Although it was the time of darkness in this strange world, the darkness at this usual hunting period was oddly pierced by the monster's hated enemy—light. The food vibrations were stronger than the shape of slime had ever experienced. They were on all sides, powerful, purposeful, moving in many directions all through the lower layers of puzzling, light-riven darkness.

Lifting out of the ooze, the hood of horror flowed up a lattice-work of gnarled swamp snags and hung motionless, while drops of muddy water rolled off its glistening surface and dripped below. The thing's sensory apparatus told it that the maddening streaks of lack of darkness were everywhere.

Even as it hung suspended on the snags like a great filthy carpet coated with slime, a terrible touch of

Slime

light slashed through the surrounding darkness and burned against it.

It immediately loosened its hold on the snags and fell back into the ooze with a mighty *plop*. Nearby, the vibrations suddenly increased in intensity. The maddening streamers of light shot through the darkness on all sides.

Baffled and savage, the thing plunged into the ooze and propelled itself in the opposite direction.

But this proved to be only a temporary respite. The vibrations redoubled in intensity. The darkness almost disappeared, riven and pierced by bolts and rivers of light.

For the first time in its incalculable existence, the thing experienced something vaguely akin to fear. The light could not be snatched up and squeezed and smothered to death. It was an alien enemy against which the hood of horror had learned only one defense—flight, hiding.

And now as its world of darkness was torn apart by sudden floods and streamers of light, the monster instinctively sought the refuge afforded by that vast black cradle from which it had climbed.

Flinging itself through the swamp, it headed back for sea.

The guard patrols stationed along the beach, roused by the sound of gunfire and urgent shouts of warning from the interior of the swamp, stood or knelt with ready weapons as the clamor swiftly approached the sea.

The dismal reedy beach lay fully exposed in the harsh glare of searchlights. Waves rolled in toward shore, splashing white crests of foam far up the sands. In the searchlights' illumination the dark waters glistened with an oily iridescence.

The shrill cries increased. The watchers tensed, waiting. And suddenly across the long dreary flats clotted with weed stalks and sunken drifts there burst into view a nightmare shape which froze the shore patrols in their tracks.

A thing of slimy blackness, a thing which had no essential shape, no discernible earthly features, rushed through the thorn thickets and onto the flats. It was a shape of utter darkness, one second a great flapping hood, the next a black viscid pool of living ooze which flowed upon itself, sliding forward with incredible speed.

Some of the guards remained rooted where they stood, too overcome with horror to pull the triggers of their weapons. Others broke the spell of terror and began firing. Bullets from half a dozen rifles tore into the black monster speeding across the mud flats.

As the thing neared the end of the flats and approached the first sand dunes of the open beach, the patrol guards who had flushed it from the swamp broke into the open.

One of them paused, bellowing at the beach guards. "It's heading for sea! For God's sake don't let it escape!"

The beach guards redoubled their firing, suddenly realizing with a kind of sick horror that the monster was apparently unaffected by the rifle slugs. Without a single pause, it rolled through the last fringe of cattails and flopped onto the sands.

As in a hideous nightmare, the guards saw it flap over the nearest sand dune and slide toward the sea. A moment later however, they remembered the barbed wire beach barrier which Chief Underbeck had stubbornly insisted on their erecting.

Gaining heart, they closed in, running over the dunes

toward the spot where the black horror would strike the wire.

Someone in the lead yelled in sudden triumph. "It's caught! It's stuck on the wire!"

The searchlights concentrated swaths of light on the barrier.

The thing had reached the barbed wire fence and apparently flung itself against the twisted strands. Now it appeared to be hopelessly caught; it twisted and flopped and squirmed like some unspeakable giant jellyfish snared in a fisherman's net.

The guards ran forward, sure of their victory. All at once however, the guard in the lead screamed a wild warning. "It's squeezing through! It's getting away!"

In the glare of light they saw with consternation that the monster appeared to be *flowing* through the wire, like a blob of liquescent ooze.

Ahead lay a few yards of downward slanting beach and, beyond that, rolling breakers of the open sea.

There was a collective gasp of horrified dismay as the monster, with a quick forward lurch, squeezed through the barrier. It tilted there briefly, twisting, as if a few last threads of itself might still be entangled in the wire.

As it moved to disengage itself and rush down the wet sands into the black sea, one of the guards hurled himself forward until he was almost abreast of the barrier. Sliding to his knees, he aimed at the escaping hood of horror.

A second later a great searing spout of flame shot from his weapon and burst in a smoky red blossom against the thing on the opposite side of the wire.

Black oily smoke billowed into the night. A ghastly stench flowed over the beach. The guards saw a flaming mass of horror grope away from the barrier. The soldier who aimed the flamethrower held it remorselessly steady.

There was a hideous bubbling, hissing sound. Vast gouts of thick, greasy smoke swirled into the night air. The indescribable stench became almost unbearable.

When the soldier finally shut off the flamethrower, there was nothing in sight except the white-hot glowing wires of the barrier and a big patch of blackened sand.

With good reason the mantle of slime had hated light, for its ultimate source was fire—the final unknown enemy which even the black hood could not drag down and devour.

Levitation

MORGAN'S WONDER CARNIVAL moved into Riverville for an overnight stand, setting up its tents in the big ball park on the edge of the village. It was a warm evening in early October and by seven o'clock a sizable crowd had made its way to the scene of raucous amusement.

The traveling show was neither large nor particularly impressive of its type, but its appearance was eagerly welcomed in Riverville, an isolated mountain community many miles from the motion picture houses, vaudeville theatres and sports arenas situated in larger towns.

The natives of Riverville did not demand sophisticated entertainment; consequently the inevitable Fat Lady, the Tattooed Man and the Monkey Boy kept them chattering animatedly for many minutes at a time. They crammed peanuts and buttered popcorn into their mouths, drank cup after cup of pink lemonade, and got their fingers all but stuck together trying to scrape the paper wrappers off colored taffy candies.

Everyone appeared to be in a relaxed and tolerant state of mind when the barker for the Hypnotist began his spiel. The barker, a short stocky man wearing a checkered suit, bellowed through an improvised megaphone, while the Hypnotist himself remained aloof at the rear of the plank platform erected in front of his tent. He appeared disinterested, scornful, and he scarcely deigned to glance at the gathering crowd.

At length, however, when some fifty souls had assembled in front of the platform, he stepped forward into the light. A murmur went up from the crowd.

In the harsh overhead electric glare, the Hypnotist made a striking appearance. His tall figure, thin to the point of emaciation, his pale complexion, and most of all his dark, sunken eyes, enormous and brilliant, compelled immediate attention. His dress, a severe black suit and an archaic black string tie, added a final Mephisphelean touch.

He surveyed the crowd coolly, with an expression betraying resignation and a kind of quiet contempt.

His sonorous voice reached to the far edge of the throng. "I will require one volunteer from among you," he said. "If someone will kindly step up—"

Everyone glanced around, or nudged his neighbor, but nobody advanced toward the platform.

The Hypnotist shrugged. "There can be no demonstration," he said in a weary voice, "unless one of you is kind enough to come up. I assure you, ladies and gentlemen, the demonstration is quite harmless, quite without danger."

He looked around expectantly and presently a young man slowly elbowed through the crowd toward the platform.

The Hypnotist helped him up the steps and seated him in a chair.

"Relax," said the Hypnotist. "Presently you will be asleep and you will do exactly what I tell you to do."

The young man squirmed on the chair, grinning self-consciously toward the crowd.

The Hypnotist caught his attention, fixing his enor-

Levitation

mous eyes on him, and the young man stopped squirming.

Suddenly someone in the crowd threw a large ball of colored popcorn toward the platform. The popcorn arched over the lights, landing squarely atop the head of the young man sitting in the chair.

He jerked sideways, almost falling off the chair, and the crowd, quiet a moment before, guffawed boisterously.

The Hypnotist was furious. He turned scarlet and literally shook with rage as he glared at the crowd.

"Who threw that?" he demanded in a choking voice.

The crowd grew silent.

The Hypnotist continued to glare at them. At length the color left his face and he stopped trembling, but his brilliant eyes remained baleful.

Finally he nodded to the young man seated on the platform, dismissing him with brief thanks, and turned again toward the crowd.

"Due to the interruption," he announced in a low voice, "it will be necessary to recommence the demonstration—with a new subject. Perhaps the person who threw the popcorn would care to come up?"

At least a dozen people in the crowd turned to gaze at someone who stood half in shadow at the rear of the gathering.

The Hypnotist spotted him at once; his dark eyes seemed to smoulder. "Perhaps," he said in a purring, mocking voice, "the one who interrupted is afraid to come up. He prefers to hide in the shadows and throw popcorn!"

The culprit voiced a sudden exclamation and then pushed belligerently toward the platform. His appearance was not in any way remarkable; in fact, he somewhat resembled the first young man, and any casual observer would have placed the two of them in the farm-laborer class, neither more nor less capable than the average.

The second young man sat down in the platform chair with a distinct air of defiance and for some minutes visibly fought the Hypnotist's suggestion to relax. Presently, however, his aggressiveness disappeared and he dutifully stared into the smouldering eyes opposite his own.

In another minute or two he arose at the Hypnotist's command and lay flat on his back on the hard planks of the platform. The crowd gasped.

"You will fall asleep," the Hypnotist told him. "You will fall asleep. You are falling asleep. You are falling asleep. You are asleep and you will do anything which I command you to do. Anything which I command you to do. Anything. . . ."

His voice droned on, repeating repetitious phrases, and the crowd grew perfectly silent.

Suddenly a new note entered the Hypnotist's voice and the audience became tense.

"Do not stand up—but *rise from the platform!*" the Hypnotist commanded. "*Rise from the platform!*" His dark eyes became wild and luminous-looking and the crowd shivered.

"*Rise!*"

Then the crowd drew in its collective breath with an audible start.

The young man lying rigid on the platform, without moving a muscle, began to ascend horizontally. He arose slowly, almost imperceptively at first, but soon with a steady and unmistakable acceleration.

"*Rise!*" the Hypnotist's voice rang out.

The young man continued to ascend, until he was feet off the platform, and still he did not stop.

Levitation

The crowd was sure it was some kind of trick, but in spite of themselves they stared open-mouthed. The young man appeared to be suspended and moving in mid-air without any possible means of physical support.

Abruptly the focus of the crowd's attention was shifted; the Hypnotist clasped a hand to his chest, staggered, and crumpled to the platform.

There were calls for a doctor. The barker in the checkered suit appeared out of the tent and bent over the motionless form.

He felt for a pulse, shook his head and straightened up. Someone offered a bottle of whiskey, but he merely shrugged.

Suddenly a woman in the crowd screamed.

Everyone turned to look at her and a second later followed the direction of her gaze.

Immediately there were further cries—for the young man whom the Hypnotist had put to sleep was still ascending. While the crowd's attention had been distracted by the fatal collapse of the Hypnotist, he had continued to rise. He was now a good seven feet above the platform and moving inexorably upward. Even after the death of the Hypnotist, he continued to obey that final ringing command: *"Rise!"*

The barker, eyes all but popping out of his head, made a frantic upward leap, but he was too short. His fingers barely brushed the moving figure above and he fell heavily back to the platform.

The rigid form of the young man continued to float upward, as if he were being hoisted by some kind of invisible pulley.

Women began screaming hysterically; men shouted. But no one knew what to do. A look of terror crept over the face of the barker as he stared up. Once he glanced wildly toward the sprawled shape of the Hypnotist.

"Come down, Frank! Come down!" the crowd shrieked. "Frank! Wake up! Come down! Stop! Frank!"

But the rigid form of Frank moved ever upward. Up, up, until he was level with the top of the carnival tent, until he reached the height of the tallest trees—until he passed the trees and moved on into the soft moonlit sky of early October.

Many in the crowd threw hands over horror-stricken faces and turned away.

Those who continued to stare saw the floating form ascend into the sky until it was no more than a tiny speck, like a little cinder drifting far up near the moon.

Then it disappeared altogether.

The Calamander Chest

"From the Indies, sir!" said the second-hand dealer, pressing his palms together. "Genuine calamander wood—a rare good buy, sir!"

"Well—I'll take it," replied Ernest Maax somewhat hesitantly.

He had been strolling idly through the antique and second-hand shop when the chest caught his attention. It had a rich, exotic look which pleased him. In appearance the dark brown, black-striped wood resembled ebony. And the chest was quite capacious. It was at least two feet wide and five feet long, with a depth of nearly three feet. When Maax learned that the dealer was willing to dispose of it for only twelve dollars, he could not resist buying it.

What made him hesitate a little was the dealer's initial low price and quite obvious pleasure upon completing the transaction. Was that fine-grained wood only an inlay or did the chest contain some hidden defect?

When it was delivered to his room the next day, he could find nothing wrong with it. The calamander wood was solid and sound and the entire chest appeared to be in fine condition. The lid clicked smoothly into place when lowered, and the big iron key turned readily enough.

Feeling quite satisfied with himself, Maax carefully polished the dark wood and then slid the chest into an empty corner of his room. The next time he changed his lodgings, the chest would prove invaluable. Meanwhile it added just the right exotic touch to his rather drab chamber.

Several weeks passed, and although he still cast occasional admiring glances at his new possession, it gradually began to recede from his mind.

Then one evening his attention was returned to it in a very startling manner. He was sitting up, reading, late in the evening, when for some reason his eyes lifted from his book and he looked across the room toward the corner where he had placed the chest.

A long white finger protruded from under its lid.

He sat motionless, overwhelmed with sudden horror, his eyes riveted on this appalling object.

It just hung there unmoving, a long pale finger with a heavy knuckle bone and a black nail.

After his first shock, Maax felt a slow rage kindling within him. The finger had no right to be there; it was unreasonable—and idiotic. He resented it bitterly, much as he would have resented the sudden intrusion of an unsavory roomer from down the hall. His peaceful, comfortable evening was ruined by this outrageous manifestation.

With an oath, he hurled his book straight at the finger.

It disappeared. At least he could no longer see it. Tilting his reading light so that its beams shot across the room, he strode to the chest and flung open the lid.

There was nothing inside.

Dropping the lid, he picked up his book and returned to the chair. Perhaps, he reflected, he had been reading too much lately. His eyes, in protest, might be playing tricks on him.

The Calamander Chest

For some time longer he pretended to read, but at frequent intervals he lifted his eyes and looked across the room toward the calamander chest. The finger did not reappear, and eventually he went to bed.

A week passed and he began to forget about the finger. He stayed out more during the evening, and read less, and by the end of a week he was quite convinced that he had been the victim of nothing more than an odd hallucination brought on by simple eye strain.

At length, at the beginning of the second week, deciding that his eyes had had a good rest, he bought some current magazines and made up his mind to spend the evening in his room.

Some time after he took up the first magazine, he glanced over at the chest and saw that all was as it should be. Settling comfortably in his chair, he became absorbed in the magazine and did not put it aside for over an hour. As he finally laid it down and prepared to pick up another, his eyes strayed in the direction of the chest—and there was the finger.

It hung there as before, motionless, with its thick knuckle and repulsive black nail.

Crowding down an impulse to rush across the room, Maax slowly reached over to a small table which stood near his chair and felt for a heavy metal ash tray. As his hand closed on the tray, his eyes never left the finger.

Rising very slowly, he began to inch across the room. He was certain that the ash tray, if wielded with force, would effectively crush anything less substantial than itself which it descended on. It was made of solid metal, and it possessed a sharp edge.

When he was a scant yard away from the chest, the

finger disappeared. When he lifted the lid, the chest, as he had expected, was empty.

Feeling considerably shaken, he returned to his chair and sat down. Although the finger did not reappear, he could not drive its hideous image out of his mind. Before going to bed, he reluctantly decided that he would get rid of the chest.

He was in sound health and his eyes had had a week's rest. Therefore, he reasoned, whatever flaw in nature permitted the ugly manifestation rested not with him but with the chest itself.

Looking back, he recalled the second-hand dealer's eagerness to sell the chest at a ridiculously low price. The thing must already have had an evil reputation when the antique dealer acquired it. Knowing it, the unscrupulous merchant had readily consented to part with it for a small sum.

Maax, a practical young man, admitted the possibility of a non-physical explanation only with reluctance, but felt that he was not in a position to debate the matter. The preservation of stable nerves came first. All other considerations were secondary.

Accordingly, on the following day, before leaving for work, he arranged with his landlady to have the chest picked up and carted off to the city dump. He included specific directions that upon arrival it was to be burned.

When he arrived back at his room that evening however, the first thing that met his gaze was the calamander chest. Furious, he hurried down the hall to his landlady's apartment and demanded an explanation. Why had his orders been ignored?

When she was able to get a word in, the patient woman explained that the chest actually had been picked up and carted off to the dump. Upon arrival

The Calamander Chest

however, the man in charge of the dump had assured the men who lugged in the chest that there must be some mistake. Nobody in his right mind, he asserted, would destroy such a beautiful and expensive article. The men must have picked up the wrong one; surely there must be another left behind, he said, which was the worthless one the owner wanted discarded.

The two men who had taken the chest to the dump, not feeling secure in their own minds about the matter, and not wishing to make a costly mistake, had returned the chest later in the day.

Completely nonplussed by this information, Maax muttered an apology to the landlady and went back to his room, where he plopped into a chair and sat staring at the chest. He would, he finally decided, give it one more chance. If nothing further happened, he would keep it; otherwise he would take immediate and drastic measures to get rid of it once and for all.

Although he had planned to attend a concert that evening, it began to rain shortly after six o'clock and he resigned himself to an evening in his room.

Before starting to read, he locked the chest with the iron key and put the key in his pocket. It was absurd that he had not thought of doing so before. This would, he felt, be the decisive test.

While he read, he maintained a keen watch on the chest, but nothing happened until well after eleven, when he put aside his book for the evening. As he closed the book and started to rise, he looked at the chest—and there was the finger.

In appearance it was unchanged. Instead of hanging slack and motionless, however, it now seemed to be imbued with faint life. It quivered slightly and it appeared to be making weak attempts to scratch the side of the chest with its long black nail.

When he finally summoned up sufficient courage, Maax took up the metal ash tray as before and crept across the room. This time he actually had the tray raised to strike before the finger vanished. It seemed to whisk back into the chest.

With a wildly thumping heart, Maax lifted the lid. Again the box was empty. But then he remembered the iron key in his pocket and a new thrill of horror coursed down his spine. The hideous digital apparition had unlocked the chest! Either that, or he was rapidly losing his sanity.

Completely unnerved, he locked the chest for a second time and then sat in a chair and watched it until two o'clock in the morning. At length, exhausted and deeply shaken, he sought his bed. Before putting out the light, he ascertained that the chest was still locked.

As soon as he fell asleep, he experienced a hideous nightmare. He dreamed that a persistent scratching sound woke him up, that he arose, lit a candle, and looked at the chest. The protruding finger showed just under the lid and this time it was galvanized with an excess of life. It twisted and turned, drummed with its thick knuckle, scratched frantically with its flat black nail. At length, as if it suddenly became aware of his presence, it became perfectly still—and then very deliberately beckoned for him to approach. Flooded with horror, he nevertheless found himself unable to disobey. Setting down the candle, he slowly crossed the room like an automaton. The monstrous beckoning finger drew him on like some infernal magnet which attracted human flesh instead of metal.

As he reached the chest, the finger darted inside and the lid immediately lifted. Overwhelmed with terror and yet utterly unable to stop himself, he stepped into the chest, sat down, drew his knees up to his chin and

The Calamander Chest

turned onto his side. A second later the lid slammed shut and he heard the iron key turn in the lock.

At this point in the nightmare he awoke with a ringing scream. He sat up in bed and felt the sweat of fear running down his face. In spite of the nightmare —or because of it—he dared not get up and switch on the light. Instead, he burrowed under the bed clothes and lay wide awake till morning.

After he had regained some measure of self-composure, he went out for black coffee and then, instead of reporting to his job, rode across town to the modest home of a truck driver and mover whom he had hired at various times in the past. After some quite detailed and specific plans had been agreed upon, he paid the mover ten dollars and departed with a promise to pay him an equal amount when the job was done. After lunch, considerably relieved, he went to work.

He entered his room that evening with a confident air, but as soon as he looked around, his heart sank. Contrary to instructions, the mover had not picked up the chest. It remained in the corner, just where it had been.

This time Maax was more depressed than angry. He sought out a telephone and called up the mover. The man was profusely apologetic. His truck had broken down, he explained, just as he was starting out to pick up the chest. The repairs were nearly completed however, and he would absolutely be out to carry off the chest the first thing in the morning.

Since there was nothing else he could do, Maax thanked him and hung up. Finding himself unusually reluctant to return to his room, he ate a leisurely dinner at a nearby restaurant and later attended a movie. After the movie he stopped and had a hot chocolate. It was nearly midnight before he got back to his room.

In spite of his nightmare of the previous evening, he found himself looking forward to bed. He had lost almost an entire night's sleep and he was beginning to feel the strain.

After assuring himself that the calamander chest was securely locked, he slipped the iron key under his pillow and got into bed. In spite of his uneasiness he soon fell asleep.

Some hours later he awoke suddenly and sat up. His heart was pounding. For a moment he was not aware of what had awakened him—then he heard it. A furious scratching, tapping, thumping sound came from one corner of the room.

Trembling violently, he got out of bed, crossed the room and pressed the button on his reading lamp. Nothing happened. Either the electricity was shut off, or the light bulb had burned out.

He pulled open a drawer of the lamp stand and frantically searched for a candle. By the time he found one and applied a match to its wick, the scratching sound had redoubled in intensity. The entire room seemed filled with it.

Shuddering, he lifted the candle and started across the room toward the calamander chest. As the wavering light of the candle flickered into the far corner, he saw the finger.

It protruded far out of the chest and it was writhing with furious life. It thrummed and twisted, dug at the chest with its horrible black nail, tapped and turned in an absolute frenzy of movement.

Suddenly, as he advanced, it became absolutely still. It hung down limp. Engulfed with terror, Maax was

The Calamander Chest

convinced that it had become aware of his approach and was now watching him.

When he was halfway across the room, the finger slowly lifted and deliberately beckoned to him. With a rush of renewed horror Maax remembered the ghastly events of his dream. Yet—as in the nightmare—he found himself utterly unable to disobey that diabolical summons. He went on like a man in a trance.

Early the next morning the mover and his assistant were let into Maax' room by the landlady. Maax had apparently already left for work, but there was no need of his presence since he had already given the mover detailed instructions in regard to the disposal of the chest.

The chest, locked but without a key, stood in one corner of the room. The melted wax remains of a candle, burned to the end of its wick, lay nearby.

The landlady shook her head. "A good way to burn the house down," she complained. "I'll have to speak to Mr. Maax. Not like him to be so careless."

The movers, burdened with the chest, paid no attention to her. The assistant growled as they started down the stairs. "Must be lined with lead. Never knew a chest so heavy before!"

"Heavy wood," his companion commented shortly, not wishing to waste his breath.

"Wonder why he's dumpin' such a good chest?" the assistant asked later as the truck approached an abandoned quarry near the edge of town.

The chief mover glanced at him slyly. "I guess I know," he said. "He bought it of Jason Kinkle. And Kinkle never told him the story on it. But he found out later I figure—and that's why he's pitchin' it."

The assistant's interest picked up. "What's the story?" he asked.

They drove into the quarry grounds and got out of the truck.

"Kinkle bought it dirt cheap at an auction," the mover explained as they lifted out the chest. "Auction of old Henry Stubberton's furniture."

The assistant's eyes widened as they started up a steep slope with the chest. "You mean the Stubberton they found murdered in a . . ."

"*In a chest!*" the mover finished for him. "*This chest!*"

Neither spoke again until they set down the chest at the edge of a steep quarry shaft.

Glancing down at the deep water which filled the bottom of the shaft, the mover wiped the sweat from his face. "A pretty sight they say he was. All doubled up an turnin' black. Seems he wasn't dead when they shut him in though. They say he must have tried to claw his way out! When they opened the chest, they found one of his fingers jammed up under the lid, near the lock! Tried to pick the lock with his fingernail, it looked like!"

The assistant shuddered. "Let's be rid of it then. It's bad luck sure!"

The mover nodded. "Take hold and shove."

They strained together and in another second the calamander chest slipped over the edge of the quarry and hurtled toward the pool of black water far below. There was one terrific splash and then it sank from sight like a stone.

"That's good riddance and another tenner for me," the mover commented.

Oddly enough however, he never collected the tenner, for after that day Mr. Ernest Maax dropped com-

The Calamander Chest

pletely out of sight. He was never seen or heard of again. The disgruntled mover, never on the best of terms with the police, shrugged off the loss of the tenner and neglected to report the disposal of the chest. And since the landlady had never learned the mover's name, nor where he intended taking the chest, her sparse information was of no help in the search.

The police concluded that Maax had got into some scrape, changed his name, and effected a permanent change of locale.

Death in Peru

HENDERSON strode impatiently down the narrow street, threading his way past patient, pannier-laden donkeys, angry, spitting, eternally incensed llamas and crowds of barefoot Indians balancing enormous baskets on their heads. He entered the open door of a flat-roofed adobe house, hurried through a single room to the patio beyond and crossed this inner court to another half-darkened adobe structure.

As his shadow fell across the threshold, a decrepit Indian woman who resembled nothing so much as a mummy appeared in the doorway.

Henderson's tired eyes sought her face. "How is he?"

The woman shifted her cud of coca leaves and shook her head. "Last night the freezing; today again the fever."

He pushed past her into the room, pausing a moment until his eyes became accustomed to the shadowy interior.

In one corner of the room a paraffin lamp spluttered ineffectually and next to it on a homemade cot Larrifer tossed and moaned as he had done for three days. He was light-headed and feverish, given to hallucinations, and he did not recognize the man who had been his close associate and business partner for half a decade.

A week before he had enjoyed vigorous good health and spirits; today he was half alive, a muttering sleepless bundle of parchment-like skin and protruding bones.

Henderson stood by the cot, scowling, studying the wasted fever-racked form. At length he turned away, inwardly cursing his luck, cursing the business venture that had brought them to the inaccessible Peruvian village. It would be days, possibly even weeks, before the runner returned with the only white doctor in the vicinity. And Larrifer was getting worse almost by the hour.

He gave some brief instructions to the Indian woman, moved at a weary gait along the sun-steeped inner wall of the patio and bent through a narrow archway which gave access to the garden in the rear of the building. Angling off the grass-grown pathway, he reached the shade of a giant araucaria tree and sat down.

The setting suited his mood. In former more prosperous days the garden had no doubt boasted delicate capuchin roses and gorgeous white trumpet flowers, but today it was the abode of dust-coated prickly pear, unsightly Indian figs and black creeping thorn thickets.

He surveyed the scene with distaste and tried to think.

At first he assured himself that Larrifer had contacted some tropical ailment, something brought on by the food or the water, or by the climate itself. But Larrifer had spent years in the tropics. And the usual medicines did not help as they had in the past. And then there was the attitude of the Indians.

Of course, he knew what they were thinking—what they were whispering among themselves. They believed that Larrifer was bewitched.

The story had had its inception two weeks before when Larrifer with his usual excess of animal spirits had become enamoured of the young daughter of a family of poor maize growers on the outskirts of the village. The girl was hardly more than a child to a white man's way of thinking, but Larrifer had experienced no great difficulty in satisfying his desires. The girl's parents, with that curious native blend of inbred fatalism and passivity, had at least outwardly consented, even if they did not inwardly approve. They were poor people and a little gold was like an immense fortune.

But it appeared that the girl had an admirer. He was a young lad, an Indian, who roamed like a vicuna in the nearby mountains and occasionally visited the village. Several days after Larrifer's little affair he had come down from the mountains with a sprig of blue snow flowers for the maize grower's daughter.

Of course he had soon learned what was on the tip of every gossip's tongue.

He had done nothing—nothing, that is, which to a white man would appear especially meaningful or sinister. He had merely loafed outside Larrifer's lodgings until Larrifer appeared. Then he had fixed on Larrifer a strange concentrated gaze, turned on his heel without a word, and disappeared.

Larrifer had been annoyed, no more. But the next day he was ill. He had been sick ever since. And he was steadily growing worse.

Henderson hated to admit the fact even to himself —but actually he was half in agreement with the Indians. He had been the unwilling witness to more than one inexplicable event during his sojourn in the tropics. There were some things he would never admit, things he disbelieved with his mind but believed with another part of himself, with his heart, with his instincts, with some primitive elemental part of his being which did not reason but merely accepted without explanation.

That night his tired brain kept on speculating even in sleep. He kept dreaming of Larrifer, Larrifer coming out of his adobe lodgings into the sun-flooded street and meeting the young Indian lad who lived like a vicuna on the mountaintops. He saw Larrifer's satisfied smile turn to a grimace of sudden irritation as the lad stared at him, saw the young Indian turn away meekly without uttering a single syllable and vanish into the crowd, saw a sprig of blue snow flowers lying unnoticed on the footstones, trampled by the throngs, withering in the sun.

The next day Henderson paid a surreptitious visit to the town's reputed sorcerer, a centenarian sandal-maker who dealt in toads' hearts and condor claws and according to local legend made a yearly pilgrimage to a shrine of the elder gods, the lost Incan deities, deep in the mountains.

The gnarled, peering ancient emerged from the rear of his shop like a reluctant spider, shading his eyes, as if the faint sunlight filtering through the dust-filmed windows was more than he could bear.

Haltingly, Henderson told his tale. He finished, hinted at the huge reward he was willing to pay for his friend's cure, and waited, hopefully.

The old man spoke at last, his voice as toneless and faraway as an evening wind rustling in distant guava trees.

"The sun burns the mountains by day; by night the mountains freeze in the wind."

He started to turn away, then added, as if with an afterthought: "Take the llama trail that leads to the top of the mountain. At the end of the path, before the snow line, the earth has been broken. There you must dig."

Henderson paid him, somewhat furtively departed, and hurried back toward his own quarters. With many misgivings, he packed a light lunch and, after stowing it in a knapsack along with a few other items, set out for the mountains. He carried a small pick in his belt and under his left arm in a hidden holster a .32 caliber automatic pistol.

He did not like riddles, and, as a matter of fact, had little real faith in the sorcerer's advice. He would never have admitted to any white man that he intended climbing to the top of a moutain on the suggestion of a Peruvian sandal-maker who worshipped the gods of the Incas and dealt in such items as toads' hearts and the preserved finger joints of suicides' hands. He would not quite admit the real object of his little jaunt even to himself. He assured himself that he needed fresh air and sunshine; he needed exercise, too. And there would be a splendid view from the mountain.

He passed the maize fields on the outskirts of the village and, after crossing a dreary plain, barren save for patches of forbidding thorn thicket, began a gradual ascent of the mountains. The foothills with their grass slopes and hidden songbirds seemed especially inviting, but as he toiled upward the grass gave way to grey lichen and at length almost absolute silence prevailed.

The llama trail led along ragged cliffs, skirting steep yawning gorges, so that prudence demanded his eyes remain ever on his feet and the better the view became the less he was able to enjoy it. Occasionally the rocks creaked in the colder air but this only accentuated the growing silence. Once a huge shadow dropped across the path and he whirled in momentary terror. The cold unswerving eyes of a passing condor stared down at him and then the majestic bird floated off across an adjacent gorge.

In spite of himself, he shuddered. He began to become conscious of a growing sense of horror. He seemed to have entered another world, a world composed of soundlessness and space, a timeless world of brooding mystery where even the eons left hardly a sign.

He recalled the sorcerous sandal-maker with a feeling of dread and began to wish he had never consulted the hoary dispenser of charms.

At length, however, he reached the end of the llama trail, which was as close to the top of the mountain as all but a vicuna might get, and recalled the words of the wizard: "At the end of the path, before the snow-line, the earth has been broken. There you must dig."

Just ahead of him the fringe of a snow-field glittered in the sun. He began to inspect the ground. Although there was no sign of any recent trespasser, neither footprints nor hoofmarks, he decided on a systematic search. Watching the ground carefully, he started near the snow-field, pacing off parallel strips.

Finally his efforts were rewarded. About three yards from the edge of the snow-line he discovered a small patch of recently disturbed earth.

As he removed the pick from his belt and began to dig, the little hairs on the nape of his neck tingled and lifted. There was something weird and uncanny about the business. How had a decrepit cobbler in the village known that at this particular spot on the mountain he would find a patch of freshly broken earth? How had he known that. . . .

He started as his pick struck into something that

was not earth. Laying the implement aside, he carefully scooped away the loose dirt with his hands.

He gasped with astonishment as the thing came into view. It was a peculiarly repellent little doll, a kind of puppet about eight inches high, moulded out of some waxlike sticky substance which was probably llama fat mixed with maize meal. Although the point of his pick had rather seriously damaged its head, there was no mistaking the crudely-shaped features. The doll's face was undoubtedly modeled after Larrifer's.

As he lifted it from its earthen bed he noticed several short hairs glued to the top of its head. Coarse, reddish-brown hairs. Larrifer's.

The sandal-maker's riddle suddenly rang in his ears with its full meaning. "The sun burns the mountains by day; by night the mountains freeze in the wind."

So that was it! Larrifer wracked with a raging fever during the day; Larrifer seized with fits of freezing by night! A puppet made in Larrifer's likeness buried on the mountain, baked by the heat of the sun during the day, frozen by the frigid winds that swept over these peaks by night!

Of course it was a coincidence, and yet. . . .

Carefully, he deposited the puppet in his knapsack, replaced the pick in his belt, and began to retrace his footsteps down the llama path. Glancing at his watch, he saw that it was just after three o'clock. He suddenly felt very much alone and began to hurry in spite of the serious consequences which a misstep might entail. He almost wished for a glimpse of the condor even though it had frightened him before. He forgot completely the lunch which he carried. There was something eerie and terrifying about these mountains. Under different circumstances he might have gloried in their grim, lonely grandeur, but the caricature of

Larrifer staring up at him out of the freshly broken earth had shaken his nerve. He fingered the butt of his pistol and more than once glanced warily over his shoulder.

Once he reached the foothills, however, his apprehension vanished. He felt ashamed of himself and smiled when he thought what an amusing little story he would someday tell at his own expense. The time a little wax doll had sent him scurrying down a mountain like a frightened child!

He decided to go at once and look in on Larrifer. For some reason he felt optimistic. Perhaps today Larrifer had thrown off the usual fever and fallen into a quiet sleep.

The minute he crossed through the patio however, he knew that something was wrong. Nearly a dozen Indians stood clustered near the open doorway of Larrifer's room. They were silent and as he approached they stiffened in expectancy.

He hurried up, glancing from one to another. "What is it?"

The old coca leaf chewer who resembled a mummy looked fearfully into the room and made a sign to ward off demons. She began to mutter unintelligibly in her native tongue.

Henderson frowned in impatience, thrust her aside and hurried into the shadowy quarters.

The paraffin lamp still spluttered in one corner of the room and as Henderson approached the cot there was revealed to him by its flickering light a spectacle which rooted him to the floor in a rush of sudden horror.

Larrifer lay dead on the cot, his skull ripped open as if by a savage blow, and on his face an expression of unspeakable terror. Blood saturated the cot and in the deathly silence Henderson could hear the drops which had soaked through drip into a pool on the floor.

At last he tore his eyes away from the ghastly scene, and gradually his initial horror and shock were replaced by gathering rage. He saw it all now! The cunning sandal-maker had deliberately tricked him! He had been sent on a charlatan's goose-chase up the mountains so that he would not be on hand to interfere when the revengeful young Indian lad crept in to kill Larrifer. No doubt the sorcerer had informed the lad soon after he left.

He rushed outside and began to shriek curses at the bewildered Indians. Clutching the aged Indian woman who had been Larrifer's designated attendant, he accused her of aiding in his murder.

His rough grasp and accusations seemed to rouse the creature out of the daze which until now had locked her tongue.

Shaking off his hand, she vehemently denied any part in the hideous business.

But Henderson was not pacified. Why, then, he demanded, had she left the premises? Perhaps if she had remained in the room—as she was being paid to do—the terrible deed might never have occurred.

But again she shook her head. She was willing to swear a sacred oath by the gods of the Incas that she had not been more than two feet from the doorway when Larrifer screamed in his last dreadful agony. No one had entered the room before that last fearful shriek; no one had quitted it afterward.

Suddenly a wild thought struck Henderson and his voice shook as he asked the old Indian woman another question.

At exactly what time, he inquired, had that terrible last scream been heard?

She crossed herself. "It was just as the bells of the church were ringing three, señor."

He stared at her, transfixed with horror, numb, sick, cold in the hot sunlight—*For Larrifer had screamed and died at almost the exact instant that Henderson's pick had crunched into the head of the little buried puppet up on the mountain!*

On the Elevator

THE STORM had been building up far out at sea since early morning; by evening the full fury of it broke against the beach fronts. Mountainous gray waves rushed up the slopes of sand, washed across the boardwalks and churned into streets which paralleled the shore. With the thundering waves came an icy rain and winds of gale velocity. As the evening wore on, the storm raged unabated. A number of the flimsier beach cottages collapsed under its impact and waves hammered at the foundations of even the sturdiest beach-front buildings. The screaming wind sounded as if it would never stop blowing. Torrents of rain mixed with sea water swirled far inland.

Somewhere at sea the violence of the storm had wrenched the rotted remains of a ship from its resting place in the ocean muck and now bits of the wreckage hurtled shoreward with the waves. Pieces of a broken spar, splintered deck timbers and brine-encrusted rags appeared along the beaches.

Whatever was cast up, however, remained totally unseen, for there was no one foolhardy enough to prowl the shore while such a storm still raged.

At eleven o'clock that evening the night clerk on duty in the lobby of the Atlas Hotel on Ocean Street seated himself in front of the switchboard and picked up a novel.

The switchboard seldom buzzed, and, due to the

storm, most of the hotel guests had already gone up to their rooms. Except for the night clerk, the lobby was entirely deserted.

Outside, the cold, wind-driven rain, blown in from the open sea, beat steadily against the pavements along Ocean Street. A curtain of raindrops ran down the hotel's plate-glass windows and at intervals a sudden savage gust of wind drove rain against the glass with a sound like water being hurled out of a bucket.

Occasionally, when the buffeting of wind was at its worst, the night clerk glanced up from his book, scowled briefly toward the darkened, storm-lashed street, and then settled back to his reading.

As he progressed past the introductory chapters of his novel, the book's tempo began to quicken and his attention became almost completely absorbed. Even when the front door of the hotel was pushed open, he did not look up.

At length, however, the draught of chill, moisture-laden air blowing into the lobby compelled his attention. Lifting his eyes from the book, he saw that the front door was wide open.

Frowning with irritation, he laid his book aside, got up and started across the lobby to close the door.

At first he thought that an unusually fierce gust of wind had somehow blown the door open. As he closed it, however, he noticed a fresh series of irregularly-shaped muddy tracks which began just inside the door and continued into the lobby.

He had not seen anyone enter the lobby and now he glanced around with some curiosity.

For a moment he saw no one at all. Then he noticed someone standing at the far end, near the self-service elevator. The person was leaning against the wall next

On the Elevator

to the elevator, apparently waiting for the lift to descend to the ground floor.

Something about the figure aroused the night clerk's interest. The man leaned against the wall as if standing upright were a distinct effort. He had an odd, limp, *collapsed* look. But perhaps that was caused by the shapeless black raincoat which he wore.

The raincoat—a shiny, black rubber affair—simply had no shape at all. It was so long it nearly touched the floor. The sleeves looked as if they were a foot longer than the man's arms inside of them.

Discounting the raincoat, it occurred to the night clerk that the man might be sick or injured—or perhaps merely drunk.

In any case the clerk felt that perhaps he ought to help the man onto the elevator and see that he arrived safely at his room. It would take only two or three minutes, and there was little likelihood that any calls would come through the switchboard in that space of time. And if one did come through, it could wait.

But for some reason the clerk hesitated. He could not have put into words any tangible reason for his hesitation. It was simply that he felt strangely reluctant to cross the lobby and escort the man in the black raincoat up to his room.

While he hesitated, the elevator arrived. The man leaning against the adjacent wall flung the door open with a swift movement, limped inside and closed the door behind him.

He had not once turned around, and when the night clerk finally arrived at the elevator and peered through the little glass window into the shaft, there was nothing in sight except the swaying steel cables.

Returning to his novel, the night clerk found that he could no longer concentrate on it. Questions about the man in the black raincoat kept entering his mind and distracting his attention. Why had the man left the hotel door wide open to the elements? How had he walked through the lobby without being seen? Why did he wear a raincoat which was much too large for him? Had he been ill, or drunk—or merely exhausted as a result of trudging back to the hotel through the sheets of cold, cutting rain?

It was nearly midnight before the clerk stopped asking himself questions about the man in the black raincoat. And then, just as he was beginning to get absorbed in the novel again, the switchboard buzzed.

A decidedly hysterical female voice smote his ear. The woman was quite obviously terrified, and very nearly incoherent, and the night clerk had difficulty in understanding her words. He gathered, finally, that she was calling from Room 311 on the third floor, that she had intended coming down to the lobby and that she had seen something on the elevator which had imbued her with pure terror.

After doing his best to reassure the woman, the night clerk promised to investigate at once and hung up.

With a feeling of guilt, he laid aside his novel and started across the lobby. It didn't require much imagination, he reflected, to picture what had happened. The man in the black raincoat had undoubtedly collapsed in the elevator and the woman in 311, chancing upon his sprawled form in the dimly-lighted lift, had been frightened half out of her wits.

After he had pushed the elevator button, the night clerk stood nervously waiting, with his hand already on the door handle. He tapped with his foot, swore, and rubbed his chin and still the elevator did not appear. Squinting through the small glass window, he

On the Elevator

saw that the thick cables were almost motionless. That meant the elevator was not in motion; it was not descending, but remained stationary on one of the floors above.

Muttering to himself, the night clerk started for the stairs. The fool woman, he decided, had probably left the elevator door ajar and thus stalled the conveyance.

Arriving on the third floor somewhat out of breath, he started down the hall toward the elevator. Then he remembered that he would pass Room 311 before reaching it and, that being the case, he thought that he might as well stop and offer the distraught female hotel guest another word of reassurance.

He tapped on the door and identified himself. There was a listening silence and he knocked again and called out, making little effort to disguise the irritation and impatience in his voice.

At length the woman inside answered in a muffled voice, a key turned in the lock and the door was opened a crack. With a face the color of white ashes, the terrified hotel guest stared out at the impatient night clerk.

"No need to be frightened," the clerk said. "A man collapsed in the elevator. Something was wrong with him when I saw him in the lobby. I'll make sure that he's not just drunk and then call a doctor."

The woman stared at him with round eyes. Her voice was just a whisper. "But—he—it—wasn't a man. It—didn't have *any face!*"

The night clerk stared back at her, a cold twinge assailing his stomach. The woman continued looking at him, wordlessly, as if she had said all that she could bear to say.

The night clerk's first impulse was to question the fear-ridden woman, but sudden anger—both at her and at himself—overcame him. Here he was listening to a hysterical woman while a man, obviously injured, lay helpless in the elevator. Probably the man in the black raincoat had struck his face in falling and the woman stepping into the dim lift had seen a spreading smear of blood instead of distinct features.

Hesitating no longer, the night clerk curtly turned away and started down the corridor toward the elevator. Behind him he heard a door quickly slammed shut and the click of a key as it was locked.

Reaching the elevator, he saw that the door was firmly closed. He gripped the handle and pulled—and nothing happened. Looking through the little window, he saw again the slowly swaying steel cables and realized that the elevator had moved up to another floor.

He stood undecided, puzzled as to what he should do. Had the man recovered after all and gone on up to his room? Or had the woman imagined the entire episode? In any case, how had the elevator moved up to another floor when only five minutes earlier it had failed to respond to the call button? If the door had been open before, and was now closed, who had closed it?

He was still hesitating when he heard a faint clash of metal echo down the elevator shaft. It sounded like the elevator door being slammed shut on a floor above. Pressing his face against the window, he saw the cable loop begin to descend.

He had just drawn back from the window when a sudden terrifying shriek rang out above. It went on and on, louder and louder, one continuous hoarse, howling cry of ultimate torment, and then there was a blur of movement in the shaft as the elevator shot past.

On the Elevator

The night clerk remained rooted where he stood, utterly unnerved by that long-drawn howl of horror which was ringing in his ears.

The terrible cry finally subsided, ending in a series of dreadful moaning gasps which seemed to arise from far below.

Doors began opening along the corridor as frightened, pajama-clad hotel guests, aroused from sleep by the fearful scream, cautiously peered out to investigate its source.

For a full minute or more the night clerk remained weakly leaning against the elevator door. Finally, as a sense of responsibility stirred in him, he turned and called down the corridor: "Will someone please telephone for the police—and an ambulance?"

When he was assured that a police car and ambulance were on the way, the night clerk retreated down the corridor toward the staircase. In response to questions, he answered only that there had been "an accident on the elevator," and he urged the uneasy hotel guests to keep to their rooms and lock their doors until the police arrived.

He descended the stairs slowly and with vast reluctance, fearful of what he might meet at every turning. He had no desire whatsoever to enter the deserted lobby on the ground floor where he had seen the man in the black raincoat waiting for the elevator.

Luckily, a police car arrived at the front door of the hotel just as he reached the bottom of the staircase.

Sheets of rain still beat against the pavements outside. When the two dampened policemen hurried in, he explained the situation as well as he could, without adding any preamble or speculation of his own.

The officers seemed singularly unimpressed. "Probably this guy you saw got sick on the elevator, couldn't get out, and started yellin' for help," one of them said gruffly. "Let's take a look in the elevator."

When the lift failed to arrive in response to the button, the night clerk peered through the little window at the cables.

"I think it's stuck in the basement," he said.

A moment later he was leading the two policemen down the basement stairs.

Switching on the dim cellar lights, he led them toward the elevator.

The little light inside the lift had gone out and as they approached they saw that the elevator door was partially open. Something black and shapeless lay on the floor, half in and half out of the lift. It was this object, apparently, which had kept the door ajar and prevented the elevator from responding to the electric call button a few moments before.

One of the policemen produced a flashlight. They saw at once that the black object was a rubber raincoat, glistening and soaked with water.

Then the patrolman directed the beam of light into the elevator and the three of them stood rigid with shock and horror.

Inside the elevator the body of a portly, well-dressed man lay in a great puddle of blood. He had been savagely attacked. His face had been slashed until his features were unrecognizable. His throat was torn, and deep ragged gashes had been made in the jacket of his smart gray tweed suit. They were so deep that they penetrated all his clothing and blood oozed up out of them. He was quite beyond help.

In spite of the obliteration of the man's features, the night clerk recognized him as one of the hotel guests, a Mr. Traverson who maintained a small suite on the fifth floor. And he was sure, he told the two police-

On the Elevator

men, that it was *not* Mr. Traverson whom he had seen wearing the black raincoat.

The night clerk believed that Mr. Traverson had gotten onto the elevator on the fifth floor, while he himself was waiting for it on the third. And he was convinced now that it was Traverson's death screams which he had heard as the elevator shot past on its way to the basement.

By the time the ambulance attendants arrived and found that they had a corpse on their hands, the police had made several startling discoveries.

The black raincoat, they found, smelled of salt water and inside it they noticed several small bits of seaweed. More pertinent, they traced a series of fresh, irregularly-shaped muddy tracks which led from the elevator, through the basement, to an areaway which, surprisingly, had been left open—or had been opened —to the driving rain. Beyond this point, due to the sweeping torrents of water, the tracks were entirely washed away.

The subsequent search and investigation uncovered nothing further. Although a cordon of police was immediately thrown about the district, no likely suspects were apprehended. Mr. Traverson, the coroner decided, had met his death "at the hands of a person or persons unknown." The black raincoat proved useless as a clue, since all the labels had rotted away from it and there was nothing in any of its pockets except scraps of seaweed and a small mussel shell. The night clerk could add nothing further to what he had already told the police, and the frightened woman in 311 could only vouch that she was sure that it was *not* Mr. Traverson, living or dead, whom she had seen in the elevator. When questioned further she invariably became semi-hysterical and would only insist that whatever she *had* glimpsed in the lift did not possess any face.

It was said that one of the younger doctors in attendance at the Traverson autopsy suggested that the savage gashes might have been made, not by a weapon, but by the claws or fangs of a wild animal, or even, he hinted, by *incredibly long and powerful fingernails*. This melodramatic suggestion was, of course, dismissed by the senior doctors who officially reported the lethal wounds as caused by a knife "or other sharp instrument."

The Atlas Hotel lost a great many regular guests—including the woman in 311—and eventually the night clerk got a daylight shift in another hotel.

When questioned by curious reporters, who for a long time refused to give up on the case, he would patiently describe the events of that shocking evening and then, when pressed for an explanation, he would shake his head and say, "Well, if you ask me, chum, that murderin' thing in the black raincoat was something dead that came up out of the sea!"

The Green Parrot

SOME YEARS AGO, finding that urban interruptions were threatening to prevent my completion of a new novel on the deadline set by the publishers I moved back to a room at the Winford Inn where I had spent the previous summer. Winford, a tiny village tucked in the northern Connecticut hills, offered very few formidable interruptions.

I arrived at the Inn during October and worked steadily until late November. At length, well pleased with my progress, I decided to take a day off.

I got into my car and drove rather aimlessly around the countryside, admiring the scenery and in general enjoying myself. Although most of the leaves were down, and in certain lights the cold hills looked rather bleak, I felt that the little excursion was doing me a world of good.

Late in the afternoon, as I was returning to Winford, looking forward to a quiet evening in my cozy room at the Inn, I turned down a narrow dirt road which branched off the main route and was reputed to be a short cut.

I immediately regretted it. The road was in a bad state of disrepair and was crowded on both sides by large overhanging hemlock trees whose branches scraped against the car.

I was just about to switch on the car lights when a large green parrot suddenly flew out of the hemlocks on one side of the road, fluttered frantically away from the windshield, and disappeared under the trees on the other side.

I was so startled I very nearly ran the car off the road. Braking to a stop, I sat staring into the woods, wondering if my eyes were playing tricks on me. If a pheasant, or woodcock, or hawk, had flapped across the road, I might have been momentarily startled, but no more. But a large green parrot, in New England, late in November. . . .

I was still scowling into the woods, when a cracked and quavering voice began calling out plaintively, "Here Toby! Here Toby!"

At first I thought it might be the parrot; then I saw a little old lady appear out of the hemlocks and step into the road. She looked around uncertainly, while a most woebegone expression came over her wrinkled face. In her shapeless housedress and funny little poke bonnet she made an odd and pathetic figure.

I got out of the car and approached her. "Your parrot," I said, "just flew across the road. He went toward the woods." And I pointed toward the clump of hemlocks where I guessed he had headed.

She stood stone still and stared at me. Apparently she hadn't even noticed my car. Finally a slow unfathomable smile wrinkled her face.

Her faded eyes sought my own. "Help me," she whispered. "Help me find Toby. I've been trying to catch him so long; I'm so tired."

It was impossible for me to refuse. Her pale eyes held such a piteous appeal—and she was so old, frail and helpless-looking.

"You'd better wait here," I said. "I'll see if I can catch him."

Without waiting for her reply, I plunged into the

The Green Parrot

hemlocks. I knew there was little time to spare. It was already twilight under the trees; in another half hour the forest would be dark.

I began calling the parrot by name: "Here Toby! Here Toby!"

From far away in the woods a faint, mocking echo came back, "Here Toby! Here Toby!"

Once I thought I caught a glimpse of the bird, high up on a branch in one of the hemlocks. But I couldn't be sure. It might have been merely a last ray of sunlight glinting briefly against a green bough.

As I moved away from the road, the hemlock forest became denser. The trees grew closer together; briars and underbrush barred the way.

Darkness closed in more swiftly than I had thought possible. With it, came cold. In spite of my exertions, I began to shiver.

When I finally stopped to catch my breath, I was, for the first time, struck with the absurdity of the situation. Here I found myself, at twilight, scrambling through brambles and briars deep in a hemlock wood which stretched for miles—in search of an escaped parrot whose owner I didn't even know!

I shrugged and turned to retrace my footsteps. While I hated to go back and admit my failure to the little old lady in the poke bonnet, I felt that I could accomplish nothing by searching further. In a very short time it would be impossible to see anything at all in the woods.

In a few minutes, however, I pretty much forgot about facing the old lady, because I realized that I was lost. I hadn't gone far from the road, but for the life of me I couldn't find it again.

It got completely dark and became extremely cold. I lost all sense of direction and although I kept assuring myself that I couldn't possibly be *very* far from the road, a kind of panic began building up in me. My thin topcoat was not, I knew, designed for overnight wear in cold November woods.

At length, purely by accident, I stumbled into the road. Luckily, the car was not far away. I climbed into it, stiff and literally aching with cold, and started the motor. As I had expected, the little old lady had left. Probably she had gone home far more concerned about the loss of her parrot than about my own failure to reappear.

Back at the Inn, I took a hot bath, changed clothes, drank a glass of brandy—and made the dining room only a few minutes late. As had been my custom since returning to the Inn, I seated myself at the table which I usually shared with Colonel Buff, Miss Grover and old Mrs. Spence.

When Colonel Buff joshed me about my late arrival, my first impulse was to answer testily. I held my temper, however, and presently when the brandy and warm food began to take effect, I decided to reveal the entire ridiculous episode from which I had so recently emerged.

I soon saw that, oddly enough, even without embroidery, my little narrative was producing an extraordinary stir. From the very start, when I first mentioned the parrot, Colonel Buff stopped eating and laid down his fork as if he didn't want to risk missing a single word. I thought old Mrs. Spence turned somewhat pale, and Miss Grover appeared unaccountably agitated. She mumbled something about snow and kept glancing at the windows.

I finished amid a strained silence. At length, Colonel Buff, after exchanging pregnant glances with Mrs. Spence and Miss Grover, cleared his throat.

The Green Parrot

"My lad," he said, "this is as good a time and place as any for you to be informed of a very peculiar and pertinent fact about your, ah, experience."

"What fact is that?" I inquired.

"You must be prepared to be startled."

"Well . . . ?"

"The fact is," he continued, "that the two chief protagonists in your recent experience—excluding yourself, of course—were—ghosts."

He nodded his head at my expression of blank amazement and disbelief.

"I know it must seem incredible to you," he went on, "but that little old lady in the poke bonnet disappeared in those hemlock woods eighty-odd years ago."

Mrs. Spence nodded, shivering. "It's a well known story hereabout," she said. "Leastways, it is to the old folks."

After dessert, Colonel Buff lit a cigar and settled back to tell the "well known" local story which I had never heard. I had, meanwhile, eaten my remaining food in such a state of suspense that I hardly tasted a morsel of it.

"The little old lady in the poke bonnet," the Colonel began, " was a spinster named Miss Meerchum. At one time her people were moderately prosperous farmers. They occupied a large tract of land bordering the hemlock woods on that dirt road which you came over.

"Well, to make a long story short, the Meerchums gradually died off until finally only old Miss Meerchum was left. She continued to live on in the farmhouse, eking out a sparse existence.

"Her only solace was a large green parrot which she kept as a pet. Being alone in the world, she became inordinately attached to the bird. It was said—and this is probably sheer nonsense—that the bird could carry on a sustained conversation and that old Miss Meerchum held lengthy gossip sessions with it. In any case, Miss Meerchum undoubtedly valued the parrot above everything else in her world.

"Well, one dismal day in late November, in the year 1868 to be exact, Miss Meerchum came stumbling into Winford in a vastly agitated state. Tearfully, she explained to the villagers that Toby, her pet parrot, had escaped into the hemlock woods. She pleaded for help in locating the prized bird.

"The local menfolk, deeply touched by her piteous appeal, organized a searching party and plunged into the woods in an attempt to retrieve the aged woman's companion.

"When they started out, the skies were somewhat overcast but there seemed no threat of imminent storm. The party—men and boys—struck boldly into the hemlocks. Apparently the search, in the beginning, was considered something of a lark.

"Toward evening, when more than half of the searchers were still far in the woods, a blinding snowstorm struck. It quickly turned into a raging blizzard. A terrific wind roared through the forest, drowning out all other sound.

"Those men and boys who had already come out of the woods were forced to return to town in order to save themselves. There was no possibility of attempting to save the others. Some of them were not found until the following spring. In all, seven men and four boys perished in the hemlock woods."

"And the old lady?" I inquired after a long silence.

"Contrary to instructions," the Colonel said, "she followed some of the searchers into the woods, calling out for her beloved parrot. She perished with the

The Green Parrot

others, and to this day her poor bones have never been located. They still lie somewhere in those woods—and whatever might remain of the parrot lies there also, for it, too, was never found."

The Colonel relit his cigar. "Since that tragedy over eighty years ago, at least a dozen different people, at different times, have reported an encounter with the little old lady in the poke bonnet. Always in the fall of the year. And, invariably, not many hours after their meeting with the pathetic apparition, a severe snowstorm has settled on the area."

Miss Grover looked toward the window. "We'll be snowed in by tomorow," she said resignedly.

When I looked outside that evening before retiring, I could see stars. I drank another brandy, shrugged, and went to bed. In spite of my experience and Colonel Buff's story-in-explanation, I slept soundly.

But the next morning when I got up, I shivered in spite of the warmth of my cozy room.

The world outside was muffled and heaped with a half foot of snow, and the flakes, driven by a howling wind, were still rushing down.

Canavan's Back Yard

I FIRST MET Canavan over twenty years ago, shortly after he had emigrated from London. He was an antiquarian and a lover of old books and so he quite naturally set up shop as a second-hand book dealer after he settled in New Haven.

Since his small capital didn't permit him to rent premises in the center of the city, he engaged combined business and living quarters in an isolated old house near the outskirts of town. The section was sparsely settled, but since a good percentage of Canavan's business was transacted by mail, it didn't particularly matter.

Quite often, after a morning spent at my typewriter, I walked out to Canavan's shop and spent most of the afternoon browsing among his old books. I found it a great pleasure, especially because Canavan never resorted to high-pressure methods to make a sale. He was aware of my precarious financial situation; he never frowned if I walked away empty-handed.

In fact he seemed to welcome me for my company alone. Only a few book buyers called at his place with regularity, and I think he was often lonely. Sometimes when business was slow, he would brew a pot of English tea and the two of us would sit for hours, drinking tea and talking about books.

Canavan even looked like an antiquarian book dealer —or the popular caricature of one. He was small of frame, somewhat stoop-shouldered, and his blue eyes peered out from behind archaic spectacles with steel rims and square-cut lenses.

Although I doubt if his yearly income ever matched that of a good paperhanger, he managed to "get by" and he was content. Content, that is, until he began noticing his back yard.

Behind the ramshackle old house in which he lived and ran his shop, stretched a long desolate yard overgrown with brambles and high brindle-colored grass. Several decayed apple trees, jagged and black with rot, added to the scene's dismal aspect. The broken wooden fences on both sides of the yard were all but swallowed up by the tangle of coarse grass. They appeared to be literally sinking into the ground. Altogether the yard presented an unusually depressing picture and I often wondered why Canavan didn't clean it up. But it was none of my business; I never mentioned it.

One afternoon when I visited the shop, Canavan was not in the front display room and I therefore walked down a narrow corridor to a rear storeroom where he sometimes worked, packing and unpacking book shipments. When I entered the storeroom, Canavan was standing at the window, looking out at the back yard.

I started to speak and then for some reason didn't. I think what stopped me was the look on Canavan's face. He was gazing out at the yard with a peculiar intense expression, as if he were completely absorbed by something he saw there. Varying, conflicting emotions showed on his strained features. He seemed both fascinated and fearful, attracted and repelled. When he finally noticed me, he almost jumped. He stared at me for a moment as if I were a total stranger.

Canavan's Back Yard

Then his old easy smile came back and his blue eyes twinkled behind the square spectacles. He shook his head. "That back yard of mine sure looks funny sometimes. You look at it long enough, you think it runs for miles!"

That was all he said at the time, and I soon forgot about it, but had I only known, that was just the beginning of the horrible business.

After that, whenever I visited the shop, I found Canavan in the rear storeroom. Once in a while he was actually working, but most of the time he was simply standing at the window looking out at that dreary yard of his.

Sometimes he would stand there for minutes completely oblivious to my presence. Whatever he saw appeared to rivet his entire attention. His countenance at those times showed an expression of fright mingled with a queer kind of pleasurable expectancy. Usually it was necessary for me to cough loudly, or shuffle my feet, before he turned from the window.

Afterward, when he talked about books, he would seem to be his old self again, but I began to experience the disconcerting feeling that he was merely acting, that while he chatted about incunabula, his thoughts were actually still dwelling on that infernal back yard.

Several times I thought of questioning him about the yard but whenever words were on the tip of my tongue, I was stopped by a sense of embarrassment. How can one admonish a man for looking out of a window at his own back yard? What does one say and how does one say it?

I kept silent. Later I regretted it bitterly.

Canavan's business, never really flourishing, began to diminish. Worse than that, he appeared to be failing physically. He grew more stooped and gaunt, and though his eyes never lost their sharp glint, I began to believe it was more the glitter of fever than the twinkle of healthy enthusiasm which animated them.

One afternoon when I entered the shop, Canavan was nowhere to be found. Thinking he might be just outside the back door engaged in some household chore, I leaned up against the rear window and looked out.

I didn't see Canavan, but as I gazed out over the yard I was swept with a sudden inexplicable sense of desolation which seemed to roll over me like the wave of an icy sea. My initial impulse was to pull away from the window, but something held me. As I stared out over that miserable tangle of briars and brindle grass, I experienced what, for want of a better word, I can only call *curiosity*. Perhaps some cool, analytical, dispassionate part of my brain simply wanted to discover what had caused my sudden sense of acute depression. Or possibly some feature of that wretched vista attracted me on a subconscious level which I had never permitted to crowd up into my sane and waking hours.

In any case, I remained at the window. The long dry brown grass wavered slightly in the wind. The rotted black trees reared motionless. Not a single bird, not even a butterfly, hovered over that bleak expanse. There was nothing to be seen except the stalks of long brindle grass, the decayed trees and scattered clumps of low-growing briary bushes.

Yet there was something about that particular isolated slice of landscape which I found intriguing. I think I had the feeling that it presented some kind of puzzle and that if I gazed at it long enough, the puzzle would resolve itself.

After I had stood looking out at it for a few minutes,

Canavan's Back Yard

I experienced the odd sensation that its perspectives were subtly altering. Neither the grass nor the trees changed and yet the yard itself seemed to expand its dimensions. At first I merely reflected that the yard was actually much longer than I had previously believed. Then I had an idea that in reality it stretched for several acres. Finally I became convinced that it continued for an interminable distance and that if I entered it, I might walk for miles and miles before I came to the end.

I was seized by a sudden almost overpowering desire to rush out the back door, plunge into that sea of wavering brindle grass and stride straight ahead until I had discovered for myself just how far it did extend. I was, in fact, on the point of doing so—when I saw Canavan.

He appeared abruptly out of the tangle of tall grass at the near end of the yard. For at least a minute he seemed to be completely lost. He looked at the back of his own house as if he had never in his life seen it before. He was disheveled and obviously excited. Briars clung to his trousers and jacket and pieces of grass were stuck in the hooks of his old-fashioned shoes. His eyes roved around wildly; he seemed about to turn and bolt back into the tangle from which he had just emerged.

I rapped loudly on the window pane. He paused in a half turn, looked over his shoulder and saw me. Gradually an expression of normalcy returned to his agitated features. Walking in a weary slouch, he approached the house. I hurried to the door and let him in. He went straight to the front display room and sank down in a chair.

He looked up when I followed him into the room.

"Frank," he said in a half whisper, "would you make some tea?"

I brewed tea and he drank it scalding hot without saying a word. He looked utterly exhausted; I knew he was too tired to tell me what had happened.

"You had better stay indoors for a few days," I said as I left.

He nodded weakly, without looking up, and bade me good-day.

When I returned to the shop the next afternoon, he appeared rested and refreshed but nevertheless moody and depressed. He made no mention of the previous day's episode. For a week or so it seemed as if he might forget about the yard.

But one day when I went into the shop, he was standing at the rear window and I could see that he tore himself away only with the greatest reluctance. After that, the pattern began repeating itself with regularity and I knew that that weird tangle of brindle grass behind his house was becoming an obsession.

Because I feared for his business, as well as for his fragile health, I finally remonstrated with him. I pointed out that he was losing customers; he had not issued a book catalogue in months. I told him that the time spent in gazing at that witch's half acre he called his back yard would be better spent in listing his books and filling his orders. I assured him that an obsession such as his was sure to undermine his health. And finally I pointed out the absurd and ridiculous aspects of the affair. If people knew he spent hours in staring out of his window at nothing more than a miniature jungle of grass and briars, they might think he was actually mad!

I ended by boldly asking him exactly what he had experienced that afternoon when I had seen him come out of the grass with a lost bewildered expression on his face.

He removed his square spectacles with a sigh. "Frank," he said, "I know you mean well. But there's something about that back yard—some secret—that I've got to find out. I don't know what it is exactly—something about distance and dimensions and perspectives, I think. But whatever it is, I've come to consider it—well, a challenge. I've got to get to the root of it. If you think I'm crazy, I'm sorry. But I'll have no rest until I solve the riddle of that piece of ground."

He replaced his spectacles with a frown. "That afternoon," he went on, "when you were standing at the window, I had a strange and frightening experience out there. I had been watching at the window and finally I felt myself drawn irresistibly outside. I plunged into the grass with a feeling of exhilaration, of adventure, of expectancy. As I advanced into the yard, my sense of elation quickly changed to a mood of black depression. I turned around, intending to come right out—but I couldn't. You won't believe this, I know—but I was lost! I simply lost all sense of direction and couldn't decide which way to turn. That grass is taller than it looks! When you get into it, you can't see anything beyond it.

"I know this sounds incredible—but I wandered out there for an hour. The yard seemed fantastically large once I got into that tangle of grass. It almost seemed to alter its dimensions as I moved, so that a large expanse of it lay always in front of me. I must have walked in circles. I swear I trudged miles!"

He shook his head. "You don't have to believe me. I don't expect you to. But that's what happened. When I finally found my way out, it was by the sheerest accident. And the strangest part of it is that once I got out, I felt suddenly terrified without the tall grass all around me and I wanted to rush back in again! This, in spite of the ghastly sense of desolation which the place aroused in me.

"But I've got to go back. I've got to figure the thing out. There's something out there that defies the laws of earthly nature as we know them. I mean to find out what it is. I think I have a plan and I mean to put it into practice."

His words stirred me strangely and when I uneasily recalled my own experience at the window that afternoon, I found it difficult to dismiss his story as sheer nonsense. I did—half-heartedly—try to dissuade him from entering the yard again, but I knew even as I spoke that I was wasting my breath.

I left the shop that afternoon with a feeling of oppression and foreboding which nothing could remove.

When I called several days later, my worst fears were realized—Canavan was missing. The front door of the shop was unlatched, as usual, but Canavan was not in the house. I looked in every room. Finally, with a feeling of infinite dread, I opened the back door and looked out toward the yard.

The long stalks of brown grass slid against each other in the slight breeze with dry sibilant whispers. The dead trees reared black and motionless. Although it was late summer, I could hear neither the chirp of a bird nor the chirr of a single insect. The yard itself seemed to be listening.

Feeling something against my foot, I glanced down and saw a thick twine stretching from inside the door, across the scant cleared space immediately adjacent to the house and thence into the wavering wall of grass. Instantly I recalled Canavan's mention of a "plan." His plan, I realized immediately, was to enter the yard trailing a stout cord behind him. No matter how he twisted and turned, he must have reasoned, he could always find his way out by following back along the cord.

It seemed like a workable scheme and I felt relieved. Probably Canavan was still in the yard. I decided I would wait for him to come out. Perhaps if he were permitted to roam around in the yard long enough, without interruption, the place would lose its evil fascination for him, and he would forget about it.

I went back into the shop and browsed among the books. At the end of an hour I became uneasy again. I wondered how long Canavan had been in the yard. When I began reflecting on the old man's uncertain health, I felt a sense of responsibility.

I finally returned to the back door, saw that he was nowhere in sight, and called out his name. I experienced the disquieting sensation that my shout carried no further than the very edge of that whispering fringe of grass. It was as if the sound had been smothered, deadened, nullified as soon as the vibrations of it reached the border of that overgrown yard.

I called again, and again, but there was no reply. At length I decided to go in after him. I would follow along the cord, I thought, and I would be sure to locate him. I told myself that the thick grass undoubtedly did stifle my shout and possibly in any case Canavan might be growing slightly deaf.

Just inside the door, the cord was tied securely around the leg of a heavy table. Taking hold of the twine, I crossed the cleared area back of the house and slipped into the rustling expanse of grass.

The going was easy at first, and I made good progress. As I advanced, however, the grass stems became thicker, and grew closer together, and I was forced to shove my way through them.

When I was no more than a few yards inside the tangle, I was overwhelmed with the same bottomless sense of desolation which I had experienced before. There was certainly something uncanny about the place. I felt as if I had suddenly veered into another world—a world of briars and brindle grass whose ceaseless half-heard whisperings were somehow alive with evil.

As I pushed along, the cord abruptly came to an end. Glancing down, I saw that it had caught against a thorn bush, abraded itself and subsequently broken. Although I bent down and poked in the area for several minutes, I was unable to locate the piece from which it had parted. Probably Canavan was unaware that the cord had broken and was now pulling it along with him.

I straightened up, cupped my hands to my mouth and shouted. My shout seemed to be all but drowned in my throat by that dismal wall of grass. I felt as if I were down at the bottom of a well, shouting up.

Frowning with growing uneasiness, I tramped ahead. The grass stalks kept getting thicker and tougher and at length I needed both hands to propel myself through the matted growth.

I began to sweat profusely; my head started to ache, and I imagined that my vision was beginning to blur. I felt the same tense, almost unbearable oppression which one experiences on a stifling summer's day when a storm is brewing and the atmosphere is charged with static electricity.

Also, I realized with a slight qualm of fear that I had got turned around and didn't know which part of the yard I was in. During an objective half-minute

Canavan's Back Yard

in which I reflected that I was actually worried about getting lost in someone's back yard, I almost laughed —almost. But there was something about the place which didn't permit laughter. I plodded ahead with a sober face.

Presently I began to feel that I was not alone. I had a sudden hair-raising conviction that someone—or something—was creeping along in the grass behind me. I cannot say with certainty that I heard anything, although I may have, but all at once I was firmly convinced that some creature was crawling or wriggling a short distance in my rear.

I felt that I was being watched and that the watcher was wholly malignant.

For a wild instant I considered headlong flight. Then, unaccountably, rage took possession of me. I was suddenly furious with Canavan, furious with the yard, furious with myself. All my pent-up tension exploded in a gust of rage which swept away fear. Now, I vowed, I would get to the root of the weird business. I would be tormented and frustrated by it no longer.

I whirled without warning and lunged into the grass where I believe my stealthy pursuer might be hiding.

I stopped abruptly; my savage anger melted into inexpressible horror.

In the faint brassy sunlight which filtered down through the towering stalks of brindle grass, Canavan crouched on all fours like a beast about to spring. His glasses were gone, his clothes were in shreds and his mouth was twisted into an insane grimace, half smirk, half snarl.

I stood petrified, staring at him. His eyes, queerly out of focus, glared at me with concentrated hatred and without any faint glimmer of recognition. His grey hair was matted with grass and small sticks; his entire body, in fact, including the tattered remains of his clothing, was covered with them, as if he had grovelled or rolled on the ground like a wild animal.

After the first throat-freezing shock, I finally found my tongue.

"Canavan!" I screamed at him. "Canavan, for God's sake, don't you know me?"

His answer was a low throaty snarl. His lips twisted back from his yellowish teeth and his crouching body tensed for a spring.

Pure terror took possession of me. I leaped aside and flung myself into that infernal wall of grass an instant before he lunged.

The intensity of my terror must have given me added strength. I rammed headlong through those twisted stalks which before I had laboriously pulled aside. I could hear the grass and briar bushes crashing behind me and I know that I was running for my life.

I pounded on as in a nightmare. Grass stalks snapped against my face like whips and thorns gashed me like razors but I felt nothing. All my physical and mental resources were concentrated in one frenzied resolve: I must get out of that devil's field of grass and away from the monstrous thing which followed swiftly in my wake.

My breath began coming in great shuddering sobs. My legs felt weak and I seemed to be looking through spinning saucers of light. But I ran on.

The thing behind me was gaining. I could hear it growling and I could feel it lunge against the earth only inches back of my flying feet. And all the time I had the maddening conviction that I was actually running in circles.

At last when I felt that I must surely collapse in another second, I plunged through a final brindle thicket into the open sunlight. Ahead of me lay the cleared area at the rear of Canavan's shop. Just beyond was the house itself.

Gasping and fighting for breath, I dragged myself toward the door. For no reason that I could explain, then or afterwards, I felt absolutely certain that the horror at my heels would not venture into the open area. I didn't even turn around to make sure.

Inside the house I fell weakly into a chair. My strained breathing slowly returned to normal, but my mind remained caught up in a whirlwind of sheer horror and hideous conjecture.

Canavan, I realized, had gone completely mad. Some ghastly shock had turned him into a ravening bestial lunatic thirsting for the savage destruction of any living thing that crossed his path. Remembering the oddly-focused eyes which had glared at me with a glaze of animal ferocity, I knew that his mind had not been merely unhinged—it had been totally destroyed. Death could be the only possible release.

But Canavan was still at least the shell of a human being, and he had been my friend. I could not take the law into my own hands.

With many misgivings I called the police and an ambulance.

What followed was more madness, plus an inquisitorial session of questions and demands which left me in a state of near nervous collapse.

A half dozen burly policemen spent the better part of an hour tramping through that wavering brindle grass without locating any trace of Canavan. They came out cursing, rubbing their eyes and shaking their heads. They were flushed, furious—and ill at ease. They announced that they had seen nothing, and heard nothing except some sneaking dog which stayed always out of sight and growled at them at intervals.

When they mentioned the growling dog, I opened my mouth to speak, but thought better of it and said nothing. They were already regarding me with open suspicion, as if they believed my own mind might be breaking.

I repeated my story at least twenty times and still they were not satisfied. They ransacked the entire house. They inspected Canavan's files. They even removed some loose boards in one of the rooms and searched underneath.

At length they grudgingly concluded that Canavan had suffered total loss of memory after experiencing some kind of shock and that he had wandered off the premises in a state of amnesia shortly after I had encountered him in the yard. My own description of his appearance and actions they discounted as lurid exaggeration. After warning me that I would probably be questioned further and that my own premises might be inspected, they reluctantly permitted me to leave.

Their subsequent searches and investigations revealed nothing new and Canavan was put down as a missing person, probably afflicted with acute amnesia.

But I was not satisfied, and I could not rest.

Six months of patient, painstaking, tedious research in the files and stacks of the local University Library finally yielded something which I do not offer as an explanation, nor even as a definite clue, but only as a fantastic near-impossibility which I ask no one to believe.

One afternoon, after my extended research over a period of months had produced nothing of significance, the Keeper of Rare Books at the University Library triumphantly bore to my study niche a tiny, crumbling pamphlet which had been printed in New Haven in 1695. It mentioned no author and carried the stark title, *Deathe of Goodie Larkins, Witche*.

Several years before, it revealed, an ancient crone, one Goodie Larkins, had been accused by neighbors of turning a missing child into a wild dog. The Salem madness was raging at the time and Goodie Larkins had been summarily condemned to death. Instead of being burned, she had been driven into a marsh deep in the woods where seven savage dogs, starved for a fortnight, had been turned loose on her trail. Apparently her accusers felt that this was a touch of truly poetic justice.

As the ravening dogs closed in on her, she was heard by her retreating neighbors to utter a frightful curse:

"Let this lande I fall upon lye alle the way to Hell!" she had screamed. *"And they who tarry here be as these beastes that rende me dead!"*

A subsequent inspection of old maps and land deeds satisfied me that the marsh in which Goodie Larkins was torn to pieces by the dogs after uttering her awful curse originally occupied the same lot or square which now enclosed Canavan's hellish back yard!

I say no more. I returned only once to that devilish spot. It was a cold desolate autumn day and a keening wind rattled the brindle stalks in that unholy acre. I cannot say what urged me back; perhaps it was some lingering feeling of loyalty toward the Canavan I had known. Perhaps it was even some last shred of hope. But as soon as I entered the cleared area behind Canavan's boarded-up house, I knew I had made a mistake.

As I stared at the stiff waving grass, the bare trees and the black ragged briar bushes, I felt as if I, in turn, were being watched. I felt as if something alien and wholly evil were observing me, and though I was terrified, I experienced a perverse, insane impulse to rush headlong into that whispering expanse. Again I imagined I saw that monstrous landscape subtly alter its dimensions and perspectives until I was staring toward a stretch of blowing brindle grass and rotted trees which ran for miles. Something urged me to enter, to lose myself in the lovely grass, to roll and grovel at its roots, to rip off the foolish encumbrances of cloth which covered me and run howling and ravenous, on and on, on and on. . . .

Instead, I turned and rushed away. I ran through the windy autumn streets like a madman. I lurched into my rooms and bolted the door.

I have never gone back since. And I never shall.

I'm Murdering Mr. Massington

HE WAS ONE of the saddest-looking men I have ever seen. I met him quite casually in a bar in Boston; after a few drinks he began to talk.

Aside from the expression of ineffable melancholy which marked his features, there was nothing impressive about his appearance. He was short and stocky, with a round face which looked fuller than it was, due to his small eyes and somewhat receding chin. Occasionally he manifested certain nervous little mannerisms, such as looking quickly over his shoulder, or suddenly clasping his hands together. He was plainly dressed in a brown suit which was neither new nor neatly pressed.

As he talked, I learned that his name was Henry Standish Massington and that he was ridden by a single, overwhelming obsession: he could not bear the thought that he would probably soon die and that thereafter no single trace of him would remain on the earth. The thought that both he and his name would be obliterated he found intolerable.

He had no heirs, no relatives at all, and he had never accumulated anything of consequence. He had no talent of any type and he did not have money enough to erect himself a monument.

He told me that at one time he was partially consoled by the thought that he could at least buy himself a modest headstone and have his name chiseled into it. But now he was convinced that the next war, with its appalling weapons of wholesale destruction, would pulverize even the granite gravestones in the city cemeteries.

He had, he admitted, considered performing some spectacular crime of violence in order to perpetuate his name, but he had finally realized that he could not bear to injure any of his fellow men. He was an atheist apparently, but a gentle one. He told me that he would like to believe in a future life, but he found himself unable to do so.

When I pointed out that his probable fate was no different from that of millions of other people who lived, died and were quickly forgotten, he only shrugged. Most of them abhorred death, he agreed, but very few seemed to care that the fact of their existence would soon be forgotten. *He* found it intolerable. It was useless for him to attempt to rationalize his obsession. There it was, and he could not rid himself of it.

At length the conversation shifted to me. When he learned that I was a writer, his interest quickened. He questioned me closely. Finally he asked if he could see some of my published work. I told him that a book of my poems was at the local public library, and that I'd gladly send him magazines which contained some of my stories, if he'd promise to return them.

He copied down my address, swore that he'd return the magazines, solemnly shook my hand and departed.

Somewhat reluctantly, I sent him the magazines as I had promised, and after a week or so he began to recede from my mind. I realized it was highly unlikely that the magazines would be returned, but since I

I'm Murdering Mr. Massington

had duplicate copies, it would be of no great consequence.

Then one evening, quite unannounced, he appeared at my apartment bearing the magazines.

I invited him in and he accepted a drink. He had, he said, read my book of poems and the magazine stories very carefully, and he was convinced that I had genuine talent. He said he was sure that a handful of the poems would survive; the stories he found uneven, but he felt that some day I would publish the best of them in a collection. At the least, he predicted, a half dozen of them would pass into anthologies.

I was pleased with his verdict and offered him another drink. He finished that and then, much to my astonishment, revealed the real reason for his interest in my work: he wanted me to write and publish a little story about him and thus preserve his name as well as some record of his personality. He was not joking; I have never seen a man more deadly in earnest.

When I told him that in spite of his opinion of my work, I was, after all, a relatively unknown writer, that he would do better to take his case to a Maugham, a Hemingway, or a Wilbur Daniel Steele, he only shrugged. He had little chance of ever meeting anyone like that, he said, and even if he did, there was no assurance that a really famous writer would cooperate with him. People who were well known, he argued, were bothered by all sorts of cranks. They had to be brushed off. He'd probably be put in the same category and never get to first base.

When I explained that even if I wrote a story I could not guarantee that it would ever be published, he shrugged again. He realized that; he was willing to take the chance, if I was. He had nothing to lose, and I would be gambling only a few hours of my time. If the story sold, I'd get some kind of a check—and he would be consoled by the thought that his name might be preserved.

It was the weirdest proposition I had ever encountered, but its bizarre nature appealed to me.

When I learned what his plans were in the event the story was published, however, I at first refused to write it. But he insisted that his plans were predetermined in any case. The publication of my story would change the time element only, and that not appreciably.

He pleaded with me; he begged me, and finally I agreed.

I imposed the following conditions: the story must be short and I would have to be granted complete freedom to write what I wished, so long as I did not change his name nor alter any of the essential facts about him. I told him that I would not flatter him by physical description or otherwise, and also I made him write out and sign a note which granted me permission to use him in a story.

He seemed quite satisfied with the terms. I told him that I would write him if and when the story was published. If he did not hear from me in a year, he was to assume that I had been unable to market the piece.

Here are a few facts concerning him which he said he would like to have included in the story. He spent most of his life plastering flowery wallpaper on rooms in the Boston area. He never married. Once he was in love with a girl named Noraline who married a Boston carpenter and later moved to Salt Lake City. He relished swordfish, mushrooms, quince jelly and cornbread (not in combination). He hated milk, cabbage and soft white baker's bread. Once he had caught a baseball fouled off the bat of Lefty Grove. He had never been arrested.

This is the story. As I write it, I have no idea whether or not it will be published. If it is, I will immediately get in touch with Henry Standish Massington. And here is what will happen.

A few hours or days before or after you read this, or possibly even as you are reading it, Henry Standish Massington—having read it—will take a cheap room in some obscure tenement in Boston, carefully destroy all evidence which might establish his identity and then, consoled by the thought that his name may possibly endure, he will sit down in a chair and calmly fire a bullet into his brain.

The Hunt

As HE ENTERED the cold dimly-lighted waiting room of the railroad station at Newbridge, Mr. Oricto decided it was the most desolate place in the world. Everything depressed him: the harsh overhead lights, the cold stone floor, the blackened uncomfortable benches.

Except for himself, the station appeared to be deserted. Frowning, he set his bag on the floor and sat down. He was late and his train was late. He would have to make the best of an hour's delay. It was a dismal prospect.

Small of frame, nervous and middle-aged, he experienced a disquieting sensation of isolation, of vulnerability, as he glanced around the big barren room. Ordinarily his rather large ears and pendulous cheeks gave him a comical appearance, but now he looked merely pathetic.

He was aware of an inexplicable feeling of apprehension. He could not account for it. Newbridge was a reasonably large town; there must be people moving about in the station area.

But it was quite late and— Suddenly he froze. Someone standing in the shadows at the far end of the room was watching him. This person was leaning against the back of one of the benches, head on arms, and he appeared to be examining Mr. Oricto with curious intensity.

Mr. Oricto's heart began pounding between his

frail ribs. He stared back fearfully, repelled yet fascinated.

Although his eyes started to water, he was unable to withdraw his gaze. As he watched, the object of his unwilling scrutiny moved along the bench and drifted into the light.

For some reason which he dared not analyze, Mr. Oricto was seized with near panic. To a casual observer there might have been little in the other's appearance to warrant such a reaction. The man was neatly groomed. He was even smaller in frame than Mr. Oricto. A disinterested party would have concluded there was nothing at all remarkable or noteworthy about him. He might even be called nondescript.

But Mr. Oricto found him appalling. The stranger's questing eyes, his look of lean muscularity and his restless, head-lifting mannerism were alarming in themselves. His quick, concentrated interest in Mr. Oricto was scarcely short of terrifying.

Without thinking, without even waiting to weigh the result of his action, Mr. Oricto grabbed his bag and hustled toward the platform door. He almost, but not quite, ran.

Hurrying to the very end of the platform, he set down his bag and looked back. He saw no one.

His heart gradually slowed in its beat. He expelled a long shaken sigh. How timid and jittery he had suddenly become! He really must get a grip on himself. He had lost sleep lately; his nerves must be a bit frayed. The stranger had probably wanted to strike up a conversation, nothing more.

But while he reasoned with himself, some secret part of him remained chilled and frightened. He could not bring himself to leave the far end of the platform.

A few drops of rain struck his face. Staring around,

The Hunt

he saw that there was no one in sight in any direction. The station might as well have been located in the middle of a wilderness. Glancing at his watch, he realized that he still had forty minutes to wait.

Rain came down harder, drumming against the wooden walk boards. A skimpy length of roof covered that portion of the platform adjacent to the waiting room, but it ended yards from the place where Mr. Oricto was standing.

As the rain increased, he began inching back toward this roof. He was almost under its sheltering edge when he saw the stranger standing just outside the waiting room doors. Mr. Oricto had not seen him come out; he had not noticed the doors swing open. But there he was, nevertheless.

Mr. Oricto stopped instantly, stricken with renewed trepidation. The lean stranger made no move toward him, but Mr. Oricto was convinced that he was being subjected to a sly and inimical scrutiny.

In spite of cold sheets of rain, flung by a rising wind, he hurried once again to the far end of the station platform.

The rain came down in torrents, soaking through his clothes, running down his face in rivulets. He felt sure that the stranger, standing dry under the platform roof, was vastly entertained by his predicament. Once he thought he heard a soft chuckle, but perhaps it was only the wind.

He could not reason with himself. His unwelcome platform companion had not actually made a single overt and hostile move or comment, yet his mere presence imbued Mr. Oricto with marrow-deep dread. The bone-chilling fear could not be analyzed away; it seemed tangible, a pregnant menace that filled the station platform like a black pall.

At intervals the rain slackened. In these brief periods of respite, Mr. Oricto shook his soaked hat, mopped the water from his face and generally attempted to regain some small measure of dignity.

In one of these intervals, as he drew his handkerchief from his face, he was horrified to observe that the stranger had left his post near the waiting room doors and advanced halfway down the platform toward him.

He stood petrified with fear. The stranger inched forward, moving his feet very slowly, very deliberately. His small head, thrust forward on a rather long neck, was pointed at Mr. Oricto like an arrow. His eyes held Mr. Oricto's in an unwavering stare.

Mr. Oricto wanted to bolt away, to leap from the platform and run blindly down the railroad tracks. That was one thing he had always been good at—running. But his legs might as well have been jelly; they could not respond to the panicky prompting of his will.

He opened his mouth to scream. Just then there was a sudden sweep of lights, a subdued roaring, and his train rushed into view around a curve.

The stranger hesitated. For one nightmare instant he seemed about to lunge forward. Then he straightened up, turned and strolled back toward the waiting room.

Never in his life had Mr. Oricto been so overjoyed to see a train arrive. He ran toward the track, grateful, inexpressibly relieved, blessing the steel behemoth sent out of the night to save him.

As he swung aboard, he shot a quick look in both directions. With immense relief, he saw that no one else appeared to be getting on.

The train did not stop long in Newbridge. It was a

The Hunt

virtual express to Porthaven and Newbridge was an unimportant stop along the way, the last stop in fact, before Porthaven. By the time Mr. Oricto got his bag in the overhead rack, the train was once again rushing through the rainy night.

He sprawled in his seat, feeling weak, chilled and exhausted. Never before had he experienced such nameless fear, such acute and overpowering apprehension. He did not dare to think what might have happened if the train had not arrived when it did.

The conductor came through the otherwise empty car, took his ticket to Porthaven, gave him a lingering, puzzled look and passed through to the next car.

The relative warmth of the train coupled with his sense of escape lulled him a little. He lay back with his eyes closed. Gradually his heart stopped hammering; he began to breathe normally again.

Rain cascaded against the train windows blurring the few lights that cut the outside darkness.

Mr. Oricto roused himself. Probably get the devil of a cold, he reflected. Well, he'd read that one should drink a lot of water for a cold. He got up, shakily, and stood in the aisle, appalled at his weakness. Making his uneven way to the water cooler, he filled a paper cup with water. After drinking three cupfuls, he swung around to return to his seat.

He stopped in his tracks. The lean stranger was lounging in a seat halfway down the car. His countenance bore an amused expression but his eyes drilled into Mr. Oricto's like needles of steel.

For a panic-filled second Mr. Oricto almost yielded to an urgent impulse. He wanted to whirl about and rush through the forward cars until he had put as much distance as possible between himself and his pursuer.

A few unaffected cells of his frightened brain assured him that he would look ridiculous. What would the conductors think? the other passengers? And what about his bag lying there in the rack? It held some of his treasured possessions. Was he going to abandon it because an unpleasant stranger was rude enough to keep staring at him?

Reluctantly, crowding down his panic, he returned to his seat. Part of his brain was still screaming at him to run, to flee while there was time, but once back in the seat, he could not bring himself to move.

Rain sluiced against the windows. Colored lights made occasional brief kaleidoscopes and then solid darkness closed in again.

Mr. Oricto sat as if paralyzed. He dared not turn his head, but he could feel the probing gaze of the other on the back of his neck. A cold shudder corkscrewed down his spine.

If only the conductor would return!

Fighting off a feeling of hypnotic helplessness which seemed to be seeping into every fiber of him, he tried to plan ahead.

When the train neared Porthaven, he would quickly take his bag and hurry to the door. He would leap off the train as soon as it entered the station, perhaps even before it stopped. Then he would run. He had no qualms about it now. He would run, furiously, unashamedly, through the station, across the street and around the corner where a taxi should be waiting. Once inside the taxi, he would be safe. He would offer the driver extra money to speed away at a fast rate. A few minutes later he would be secure in his rooms.

Once his plans were formulated, he felt better. Then a new idea struck him and fear returned. Did he imagine it, or was the other actually reading his thoughts? Was everything going on in his head quite apparent?

The Hunt

Were those unwavering eyes drilling right through his skull into the secret area of his mental processes?

Mr. Oricto felt that they were. Growing fear harried him, yet he could think of no alternate plan. He would have to depend on his speed, on his fleetness afoot. There was a good chance that he would make it.

As the train neared Porthaven, he got up and lifted his bag from the rack. He stood trembling as the express shot toward the station. He knew the other's eyes were fastened on him. A wave of panic, of terrifying weakness, swept over him.

Will power alone drove him on rubbery legs to the train door. The station slid into view. He was down the metal steps. He leaped. The inertia of the moving train spun him around. Fighting to hold his bag and maintain his balance, he did a grotesque little jig.

Straightening out of it, he glanced fearfully up the platform. The lean stranger had already left the train. He was coming swiftly down the boardwalk.

If Mr. Oricto had previously entertained any desperately-cherished doubts as to the stranger's interest in his own person, they were now instantly dispelled.

He bounded toward the platform stairs.

Hurtling down the steps four and five at a time, he reached the bottom and whirled into the long feebly-lighted tunnel which connected the platform with the station proper.

Pure terror tore at him. Rushing down the tunnel, he burst through the end doors into the station. It appeared to be entirely deserted. Not even a late sweeper was in sight; half the lights were off. There could be no sanctuary here.

Bolting toward the street doors, he heard the tunnel doors crash open behind him.

He reached the street, slippery with rain, and sprinted for the corner where a taxi should be waiting. As he neared the corner, a great dread took possession of him. This one time there would be no taxi! He would round the corner and find nothing!

He had to take the chance now. He ran, wildly.

Skidding around the corner, he saw the taxi. Groaning with relief, he shot toward it. A twist of the door handle and he was inside.

The driver sat squinting at a racing form. He appeared not to have noticed that Mr. Oricto had entered the cab.

Mr. Oricto gasped out his destination. "573 Bishop Street, driver! And please hurry!"

The driver looked up from his racing form. He turned a morose, lantern-jawed face toward Mr. Oricto. There was an unspoken rebuke in his glance.

Mr. Oricto was about to make his offer of money when the door on the opposite side of the cab was yanked open.

The lean stranger slid inside, slammed the door, and spoke softly to the driver.

The driver nodded, turning toward Mr. Oricto. "You mind another fare, buddy? Only cab around this late. And it's rainin'."

Mr. Oricto sat speechless, rigid, naked fear like a knifethrust in his heart.

The driver mistook his silence for reluctant acquiescence. Muttering to himself, he thrust his racing form into the glove compartment and started the cab.

As the taxi splashed through the dark, deserted streets, Mr. Oricto sat staring straight ahead. He dared not move even his eyes so much as a fraction of an

The Hunt

inch. For blocks he sat motionless, feeling the other's eyes inspecting him, gloating, triumphant.

Finally coherent thought returned. Could he tell the driver to take him to the police station? He felt convinced that for some reason of his own the driver would not do so. What pretext could he give? And suppose the driver did bring him to the police? What could he say? That he was being followed? Would they believe him? It would seem absurd. He could prove nothing. The stranger, he was sure, would suavely sidestep any such situation. He himself would become an object of suspicion. They might even hold him as a mental case.

Despair overcame him. But as the darkened, rain-swept shop fronts moved in and out of his range of vision, one thought became uppermost: at all costs he could not let the stranger know where he lived.

Once his decision was made, he knew he would have to force himself to act immediately. Otherwise, what little strength he had left would slip away.

Scrabbling for his wallet, he told the driver to stop. His voice came out so weak, nearly a block rolled past before the driver heard his desperately repeated commands and steered toward the curb.

The driver's morose, accusing face turned toward him questioningly.

"I—changed my mind," Mr. Oricto explained in a whisper. He handed the driver a bill. "Keep the change." He wrenched open the door and ran. Not once had he dared look toward the lean stranger.

The rain had stopped. A heavy mist was settling over the streets. It lifted from the pavements like wet smoke, obscuring vision.

As he raced through the mist, Mr. Oricto remembered that he had left his bag in the cab. He hardly cared now; he could run faster without it.

He had planned to enter a bar or restaurant which was still open, but now he saw with a fresh throb of fear that it was far later than he had realized. Every establishment was closed. The streets were utterly forsaken.

When he finally slowed to a walk, he was gasping. Out of condition. Why, that was strange. All his life he had been able to run, run effortlessly almost. Almost—

He stopped to listen. Behind him in the mist he heard the swift pad of approaching feet. They were running.

He bounded forward, sprinting faster than before. Pure terror drove him on. His legs worked like pistons.

But he was already out of breath; even stark terror could supply only so much animal energy.

He knew that his pursuer was gaining. As he rushed toward an intersection, he decided to turn at right angles. Perhaps, if he wasn't seen. . . .

Just as he pivoted to turn, he shot a frenzied glance backwards.

The face of the lean stranger arrowed through the mist. He was running smoothly, head thrust forward. With a thrill of absolute horror, Mr. Oricto thought of a weasel he had once seen streaking through the woods in pursuit of some small animal.

Even as he turned the corner, he felt his maneuver had been detected. The sight of his fearful follower, however, impelled him to a new burst of speed.

The area he had turned into was more deserted and desolate than the previous one. Dark, rubbish-littered alleys opened on every side. Warehouses and abandoned, windowless tenements lined the narrow street.

Mr. Oricto's blood was pounding in his head. He

The Hunt

felt dizzy, weak. He knew he would drop if he kept on running.

There was one last, desperate chance. Without daring to look around, he darted into a black alleyway. Halfway down he slammed into an empty crate, jagged with protruding wires, and skidded to his knees. Instead of getting up, he hopped on hands and knees and hid behind the crate.

The quick pad of footsteps approached, paused for a terror-filled instant and passed.

Mr. Oricto was just beginning to hope when they returned. They came softly down the alley toward the crate. He crouched helplessly against the wall while his heart thundered and all hope drained out of him.

The lean stranger bent above him, head thrust forward and down, eyes shining.

Even in his despair, a question nagged at Mr. Oricto. He could not put it into detailed words. All he managed was a faint whisper: "Why?"

The stranger looked down at him with something like mild surprise.

"Why?" he repeated. "Why?" He lifted his small neat head and chuckled with glee. His teeth gleamed.

"Why?" he said again, lowering his head. "Because you're a rabbit—*and I was born to hunt rabbits!*"

Mr. Oricto tried to scream but only a thin bleat of terror came out of his mouth.

An instant later the stranger's pointed teeth flashed toward his jugular.

The Mail for Juniper Hill

DAVE BAINS gave me the facts last year, only a few months before he passed away peacefully in his sleep. He was ninety-two when he died and he had been retired from the Juniper Hill Postmastership for over twenty years.

I knew him for over a decade; during that time he told me many anecdotes about the early history of Juniper Hill. In every instance, where verification was still possible, I found his information fully authenticated.

Forty years ago—the time Dave Bains spoke of— Juniper Hill was an isolated Connecticut village with scarcely fifty inhabitants. You reached it by a narrow twisting "mountain" road which ran the twenty-odd miles from Grangeville through deep hemlock woods. It was a hazardous road: a ribbon of treacherous mud in the spring, a nearly obliterated trace when winter snow swirled down through the hemlocks.

Vehicles along the road were scarce enough to cause comment, but there was one conveyance which traversed the road daily in spite of mud or snow. That was Ed Hyerson's Model-T, which carried the mail to and from Grangeville. In those far days the natives persisted in referring to Ed's Ford as "the stage"—a quaint anachronism having its roots in the previous century when the mail actually was conveyed by stagecoach.

"Big Ed" Hyerson was, Dave said, "a case." He was in most respects Juniper Hill's ne'er-do-well, a hard-drinking, skirt-chasing rascal.

But Ed had one redeeming feature: he was always faithful to the Mail. No matter how much hard cider or apricot brandy he'd absorbed the night before, he would show up at the Juniper Hill Post Office on time the next day.

At the period Dave Bains spoke of, Ed had been driving "the stage" for nearly ten years and never once during that period had he failed to finish his run. On a few occasions he had been late, but that was all.

Ed was inordinately proud of his record. In his own mind it was probably the one thing which justified his existence. It fortified his ego and maintained his self-respect. He boasted about it, loudly and continually. Although no one denied his claim, there were many who wished he would let his performance speak for itself.

He was in his late thirties at this time, sturdy and strong as a bear. He flipped the heavy mail sack about as if it had been a bag full of confetti.

One freezing winter night early in December, it began to snow. By morning it was snowing so hard the big spruce wood north of Juniper Hill was blotted from sight. The wind arose, piling the gritty snow into the beginnings of formidable drifts.

Ed Hyerson drove off for Grangeville on schedule. Although the snow fell faster than ever, he returned two hours later with the morning mail. Tossing the mail sack onto the Post Office porch, he gave Dave Bains a sly wink and drove off, shouting back that he was going home to get some proper "warming medicine."

The Mail for Juniper Hill

By noon the storm had assumed all the aspects of a blizzard.

When Ed Hyerson reappeared at the Post Office to make the early afternoon pickup, Dave Bains was worried. He knew how bad the storm had become—and he also knew how stubborn Ed Hyerson could be.

Big Ed had been drinking. He burst into the Post Office with an Iroquois war whoop and slung the mail sack over his shoulder.

Dave rose from his creaky chair behind the sorting rack. "It's pretty bad, Ed. You think you'll get through?"

Slamming down the mail sack, Ed scowled at Dave as if the old man had suddenly lost his wits. "Git through?" he repeated. "You think a little snow can stop me? I been makin' this run nigh onta ten year—and I ain't been stopped yet! I reckon I ain't bein' stopped today neither!"

Talcott Willson, an old farmer who was warming his heels in the Post Office, spoke up. "Maybe you'll get down to Grangeville, Ed, but you won't get back. You'll be takin' that north wind and drift right in your teeth!"

Willson's words seemed to drive Ed Hyerson into a rage. The liquor was working in him, of course, and now he was seized with fury because Willson doubted his ability to drive to Grangeville and back in the blizzard.

Snatching up the mail sack with an unprintable oath, he glared at the two men. "I'll have the mail back here today, with Christ's help—or the Devil's. I'll bring the mail from Hell, need be!"

So saying, he stamped out, hurled the sack into the Ford, and drove off.

Talcott Willson scrubbed his chin wryly. "I still say he ain't gonna make it."

Dave Bains frowned. "Trouble is, he's crazy enough to try. If he don't get back, he can't brag about his record any more."

He sat down, fretfully shuffling papers on his desk. "I'll 'phone Fred Quender at Grangeville. Maybe Fred can talk sense enough to make him stay over—*if* he reaches Grangeville, that is."

From Grangeville, Postmaster Quender promised to do his best to persuade Ed Hyerson to remain over night, if and when he arrived.

It was not until four o'clock that Quender called back. Cursing, roaring, and reeking with liquor, Ed Hyerson had driven into Grangeville two hours late. Now, in spite of all Quender could say to dissuade him, he had picked up the return mail and started back.

The storm grew steadily worse. Snow built up in great slanting drifts. The wind shrieked without interruption.

At six o'clock, when Dave Bains again tried to telephone Grangeville, the line was dead.

Morgan Rayler, who boarded with him in the living quarters adjoining the Post Office, nodded. "I knew that line couldn't hold up against such a wind."

Dave pressed his face to the window. "Black as the bottom of a well." He sighed. "Another hour out there, and he'll freeze to death."

A probing finger of wind made the kerosene lamp flicker. Rayler waited until shadows stopped leaping in the little mail room. "Maybe," he said, "Ed headed back to Grangeville."

Dave Bains sat down. "He didn't. He won't. I know him. Big Ed will keep coming toward Juniper Hill till

The Mail for Juniper Hill

the car gets stuck. Then he'll most likely try to push it the rest of the way!"

"He wouldn't be back till seven anyway," Rayler pointed out. "Took him three hours to reach Grangeville this afternoon."

Someone knocked on the door. They both jumped.

Talcott Willson, whose farmhouse lay only just across the road, came in, scattering snow. The buffeting wind almost blew out the lamp.

Willson shut the door with an effort and took a deep breath. "Wust wind I remember," he said. "Pulls your breath away." He reached for a chair. "Wonder how Ed's makin' out?"

Dave Bains shrugged. "He started up from Grangeville. Morgan thinks he might have gone back, but the line's down."

"If he had any sense," answered Willson, "he'd never have left here in the first place!"

For a time the three men sat silent. Snow clicked against the frosted panes. The old house shook and rattled in the wind.

Dave arose finally, opened the stove and dropped in another massive maple chunk. "Seven o'clock," he observed.

"You think," Rayler asked, "he could hold out till mornin' in the stage?"

Talcott Willson looked up. "He'd freeze to death long before mornin'."

Dave paced the floor restlessly. "Maybe those big hemlocks, close along the road, keep down the drifts."

Nobody said anything and he sat down again.

By eight o'clock they had begun to stop listening. Rayler walked to the window and looked out. "You think we could push down the road a mite?"

"You git outside the village," Willson told him, "you

can't even find the road. Turn around twice and you're lost."

Nine o'clock came and went. Dave got up and put the big enamel coffeepot on the stove.

The three men drank coffee in silence, grateful for its warmth. In spite of the glowing stove, the wind sent icy emissaries through a hundred hidden apertures.

Conversation resumed and then ceased again as the hands of the big clock inched past ten.

Eleven o'clock came and went.

It was approaching midnight when Talcott Willson finally stood up. He voiced the thought of all of them. "We'll never see Big Ed Hyerson here tonight. Nearly eight hours since he left Grangeville. Either he went back or—"

He stopped short at the sound of a heavy thump on the veranda outside.

The three men stared at one another, speechless. Finally Dave Bains rushed across the room and flung open the door.

At first he saw nothing. A moaning wind tore at him; snow stung his face. He glanced down.

There at his feet lay something bulky, completely sheathed in ice and frozen snow.

It was the mail sack.

Willson and Rayler crowded behind him in the doorway. The kerosene lamp in the little Post Office room flickered out in a plume of soot. The wood stove, emitting a dim red glow, furnished the only remaining light.

For a long half-minute the three men stood gazing down at the ice-coated bulging sack. Beyond the veranda was blackness.

It was Dave Bains who walked to the edge of the

The Mail for Juniper Hill

veranda and saw the deep dragging footprints which came to the porch and turned away again.

He sprang from the veranda and stumbled forward through the drifts. A few yards ahead, scarcely visible in the thick swirling snow, someone was retreating slowly down the drive toward the main road.

Dave cupped his hands to his mouth. "Ed! Ed Hyerson! Come back!"

The figure neither stopped nor turned. With a kind of inexorable purpose it plowed stiffly on.

Dave hurried back to the veranda where Willson and Rayler waited.

"He's out there!" he told them, rushing past. "Get your coats!"

In the dimness of the red-lit room the three of them put on their greatcoats.

"Something's happened to him," Dave explained. "Mind's wandering, likely."

As they struggled down the drive, Willson looked around in bewilderment. "Where's the stage?"

"Not here," Dave replied shortly. "He must have walked in."

The booming wind snatched at their breaths as they lurched forward. At the end of the drive where the road began, they paused, peering through the snow-driven darkness.

Again it was Dave Bains who glimpsed someone moving up the road toward the center of Juniper Hill.

They lunged after, pushing into the drifts. Once more Dave cupped his hands and shouted Ed Hyerson's name. Big Ed paid no attention. With the abrupt regular motions of something mechanical, he beat his way forward.

But they began to close the gap. They were rested;

they had not been out in the freezing wind for hours.

As they advanced Dave recognized the heavy plaid muffler which Ed Hyerson wore.

Dave called his name again when they were only scant yards away.

Suddenly Ed Hyerson stopped. He stood still. Very slowly, with movements which seemed strangely wooden, he turned around.

He looked at them.

They froze into immobility, stricken cold by a deadly chill which was not of the storm.

The eyes looking at them were terrifying eyes, red with fire. They were not Ed Hyerson's eyes, for all that they looked out of his head.

Although he made no move toward them, the fixed gaze of his flaming eyes expressed incalculable menace. For a terror-filled interval, while they stared back with speechless dread, he watched them. Only his fearful eyes in all his bulk, seemed alive.

Then he turned, stiffly, with the movements of a marionette, and resumed his jerky forward march, impelled by a power greater than his own.

The three men saw him start across the village common toward the white clapboard church.

Talcott Willson gasped. "He can't—he can't want to go in *there!*"

Willson was right. Before he reached the church, Big Ed veered abruptly, heading toward the cemetery.

They watched him push toward the cemetery gate. After that, blowing snow hid him from sight.

Numbly, the three of them turned and started back toward the Post Office.

The mournful wail of the wind seemed to possess the earth.

Two days later, after the blizzard stopped, they

The Mail for Juniper Hill

found Ed Hyerson's frozen corpse at the far end of the cemetery, huddled under feet of snow. His empty Ford, buried in a huge drift, was located half way between Grangeville and Juniper Hill.

The Ballantine Horror Series

377K THE SOUND OF HIS HORN   Sarban

"... A stunning tour-de-force, a horror thriller with depth."—The New York Times.

380K TALES TO BE TOLD IN THE DARK
                                    ed. Basil Davenport

Superb knee-weakeners by the horror masters.

431K THE DOLL MAKER   Sarban

A young girl is led slowly, gently into a vortex of horror.

458K SOME OF YOUR BLOOD   Theodore Sturgeon

Psychosis: unclassified; Behavior: dangerous.

466K THINGS WITH CLAWS ed. Whit and Hallie Burnett

Terrifying tales of clawed creatures with murderous motives.

508K NIGHT'S BLACK AGENTS   Fritz Lieber, Jr.

Modern horror stories of the terror that lurks in great cities.

522K TALES OF LOVE AND HORROR   ed. Don Congdon

Twelve stories of the thin line between Love and Hate.

574   ZACHERLEY'S VULTURE STEW

A concoction of horror, spiced with the ghoulish humor that makes Zacherley unique.

Send check or money order—no stamps, please

**DEPT. 587, BALLANTINE BOOKS, INC.
101 Fifth Avenue, New York 3, N. Y.**